# The Purloined Pony

## Book 1: The Pitchfork Princesses

by

## Brenda Barnes

Pitchfork Princesses

First Mass Market Printing: July 2017

Print Edition: ISBN-13: 978-1547251117  ISBN-10: 1547251115

*This book is dedicated to my wonderful niece, Emily, who shares her eccentric aunt's love of horses. She and her barn friends and their silly antics served as the inspiration for this book.*

*I also dedicate this book to all Pitchfork Princesses everywhere, who, along with their instructors, do the hard work required to keep our equestrian passion alive and well.*

*This dedication would not be complete however, without thanking those who are unable to pick up this book and read it, specifically, the horses… our partners in this dirty, smelly, expensive, back-breaking, but oh so wonderful horsey life. Without the horses, none of this would be possible.*

www.pitchforkprincesses.com

# Chapter 1

"We were being watched." Beth pointed towards the end of the long driveway to the gates at the entrance of her aunt's farm, Wildwood Stables.

Her aunt Jayne paused the horseback riding lesson she was teaching to look in the direction Beth was pointing.

"Someone on a bicycle was under the tree watching us."

"Well you know that happens from time to time. It was probably someone thinking about lessons and wanting to check us out."

"No Aunt, this person made me feel creepy. I don't know how or why, but I just get a feeling that there was something wrong about it, and this isn't the first time this person has watched us."

This made Jayne feel concerned. "Was it a man?"

Beth shook her head. 'No, I think it is a girl, maybe my age or a little younger."

Jayne let out her breath and wiped away a trickle of sweat on her neck, "well that makes me feel better. It was probably nothing," but even as she said that, Jayne felt the flesh on her arms prickle into goosebumps on this very warm April afternoon. There was definitely something that felt wrong. A quick look about a quarter mile up the road showed a quickly retreating bicyclist frantically pedaling away. Jayne's farm was at the end of a dead-end road so it never had much traffic.

It was easy to notice anyone coming up the road and people often would drive up to check the place out. This particular person, took off as soon as they were noticed. This was certainly an odd occurrence.

"Back to work girls." Jayne called the Saturday afternoon horseback riding lesson back to order. This group of girls was her newly formed weekender club who referred to themselves as The Pitchfork Princesses. They were her most dedicated and most eager riders who she allowed to hang out and help her work on the weekends by mucking stalls and doing assorted tasks and the group included her niece, Beth.

The group of girls put their horses back to work on the dirt track that ran along the arena fence.

"Don't slouch Evelyn, lift your rib cage up.....Sarah keep those heels down and don't you dare point your toes out.....Susan, relax your hips and you will not bounce so hard on the saddle.....Monica, don't let your horse wander into the middle, get him back on the rail ...Melissa, close your fingers or that horse will get rein away from you......Beth, your horse is over flexed and you need to use more leg to push his body up to the bridle."

The girls were working hard at their lessons and Jayne was working hard at her teaching. Teaching riders and training horses required a great deal of thought. Sometimes even hours after a lesson was over, Jayne would mentally still be working out issues in her brain.... she would wake up at night with an idea about how to help a rider improve his or her riding or how to get a horse through a specific training challenge. Sometimes her brain just wouldn't shut off and she kept a little spiral-bound notebook in her farm house to jot down her ideas as she thought about them.

This spying bicyclist bothered her though. She would have to jot down a note in her notebook. Beth had said this was not the first time this bicyclist had watched, so this person would be back. Maybe if she could keep track of sightings she could find a pattern.

Jayne watched as Beth trotted by on Gus. Beth was sitting deeply wearing her favorite beige schooling breeches with camouflage knee patches, her tall black field boots and a camouflage top. She was riding strongly with her seat and had just enough squeeze from her leg muscles to push Gus up into the bridle for a brilliant extended trot. Gus was working with his neck arched, his ears pricked up and he was popping his knees up before extending his white legs forward. He just seemed to float over the ground as he went by; his almost white mane and tail rippled in the breeze behind him as his fiery copper colored coat glistened in shades of red and gold in the April sunlight.

Gus was a Morgan horse and was a small one at that. He was right at that size that was just under what was considered horse-sized. He was 14 hands and almost 2 inches tall when barefoot. At that size, he measured as a pony and he was shown in the large pony classes in the local jumping shows. Beth would soon outgrow him and her aunt already had a new horse for Jayne to begin working with for next year's show season.

As this was probably going to be Beth's last year showing Gus, she was wanting to take him to the Morgan Grand National and World Championship show for their 'Grand

Finale' together in October; afterwards he would become a lesson pony for Jayne to use for teaching lessons. He would probably also be handed down to Beth's little sister when she was old enough.

"Beth, are you forgetting something?" Jayne asked. Beth glanced at her pony's shoulders and then sat a double bounce to change her diagonal. "You gave such a brilliant extended trot, but you went twice around the arena posting to the wrong diagonal. I was waiting to see how quickly you would realize it but you forgot to check."

It was not like Beth to be that careless. When riders performed a posting trot, they were supposed to post in rhythm to the horse's shoulder that was next to the arena fence. Jayne could tell that the appearance of the bicyclist must still be bothering her if she had forgotten to check that one simple thing.

Jayne took another glance down the road before sitting down in the center of the arena on the black mounting block that riders used to get on their horses. She pulled down the brim of her hat to shade her eyes and carefully watched her riders as they rode around the arena. This group of girls on her string of lesson horses was a mixed group of English riders and one Western rider.

Little Monica was Jayne's youngest rider, and the only Western rider of the group. The idea of Monica riding Western made Jayne smile. Western Pleasure was slow and controlled and is not what Jayne thought little Monica would be attracted to. Monica was a perpetual ball of bouncing energy and Jayne thought she would have gravitated towards riding that was a little more energetic, but Monica liked the idea of wearing sparkly outfits and could only do that in Western. This six year old was all about the sparkly stuff.

Underneath her helmet, Monica's dark brunette ponytail swung back and forth in motion with her mount's slow Jog. Too slow...he was about to fall out of his jog into a walk. "Monica, a little more squeeze from your leg please."

"Mrs. Jayne, you made a rhyme!"

"Yes, I suppose I did, but I don't see you using your leg."

Jayne watched one of the lesson horses try to come off of the rail; Sarah DelRizzo was riding and she was over-steering the horse to the right in an attempt to put her back to the dirt track next to the arena rail, but the horse kept drifting her body left towards the middle of the arena. "Sarah, straighten her out and press your left leg a little more firmly; I want you to hold gently with the right rein but use your left rein to keep her straight. The best way to keep her next to the rail is to keep her straight using both your hands and legs together. You can't just pull her to the rail. Now ride her a little deeper into that corner and use hands and legs together to ride her straight, not just your right rein to keep her on the rail."

Sarah nodded and guided the horse as instructed. Sophie was her favorite lesson horse, specifically because this leggy mare was a little more challenging. One would almost say the horse had a sense of humor and enjoyed being a little bit difficult just to keep things interesting.

Jayne made a mental note to think about putting Evelyn on Sophie for a few lessons. Evelyn Knight was a beautiful and elegant rider who was ready to move up to more difficult horses, but would sometimes get frustrated if the horse wasn't perfect. Yes, she nodded to herself. Evelyn needed to ride Sophie; she would learn patience and would have to put a little more thought into her ride.

The group of girls, six in all, carried on with Jayne calling out instructions and then Jayne had them finish by coming into the center and lining up side by side. "Melissa, sit up straight.…. Susan, pull your leg back a little bit."

"Oh!" Exclaimed Evelyn as the horse she was riding, Magic, stretched out lower to the ground and began to pee. "Well I am glad he is doing that out here; I just cleaned his stall and put fresh bedding in today." The girls laughed and little Monica giggled.

Jayne opened the gate and the girls on horseback filed past on their way back to the barn. She hesitated and turned to look back down at the end of the road. The bicyclist had long disappeared but the situation was puzzling. Beth stopped her pony. "Something isn't right. I just feel that whoever that is she is up to no good, Aunt."

"You said you have seen her do this before, do you remember when it started or how often you see her here?"

"I started seeing her months ago, but it was just every once in a while, but this is the third weekend in a row she has been there watching us, and she is watching us longer now."

"Well, maybe she is just a kid from the neighborhood that wants to ride and doesn't have the money or opportunity, so she just watches."

"That is what I used to think, but something just doesn't feel good about it."

Jayne put her hand on Beth's thigh and nodded. "I know, my intuition is telling me there is something odd about it too. Well, let's get to the barn, the girls are all waiting on you to take them out on the trails for a little bit. Keep them slow, the horses worked hard today and it is starting to get hot."

Beth grinned. "They haven't been on the trails for a while; the horses will enjoy a walk off the farm."

"Yes, they will be happy to see something other than the inside of the arena; so, let's get going so you can be back before dark, and of course I don't want anyone to go past the gate on the ranger road. Stay on the trails on this side of the preserve."

They walked into the barn and Jayne told the girls the instructions she had given Beth. They all paused to allow the horses to slowly sip just a little water before they headed out, but not too much, as too much cold water in a hot horse could make them sick.

"Oh, and I am ordering pizza tonight so decide on what you want me to order." Mrs. Jayne's husband was out of town this weekend so Beth had asked if the girls could all spend the night. This seemed to have the girls all feeling a little more energetic all day long. They had rushed through their assigned work during the day so they could finish early enough for this little trail ride afterwards.

One by one, the girls put their helmets on and brought the horses out of the stalls again. They mounted up and headed down the long driveway of Wildwood Stables. They were all chattering excitedly and she smiled as she heard Sarah loudly exclaim, "we are finally out of here!" Her soft-spoken twin sister, Susan, said something Jayne couldn't hear and then they seemed to argue. Jayne shook her head when she heard little Monica call Sarah a 'poopy-head' and then Beth shushed them all as they turned left at the end of the driveway and rode along the side of the road.

# Chapter 2

The Wildwood Preserve was behind their farm to the north, and the three-thousand-acre wilderness area was divided into three sections with an entrance at both the Western side and the Eastern side of the sprawling rural neighborhood. Fortunately, Wildwood Stables was just around the corner from the Western entrance to the trails. The girls had to ride down the street and around the corner to their western entrance but fortunately, all the roads in their rural community were dead ends, so any traffic was highly unusual and the neighborhood streets were usually full of riders on horseback, kids on bicycles or scooters, and an occasional golf cart.

The girls, led by Beth, walked down the road and entered the preserve. As they walked the worn trail through the grass, they planned on what they would do on the sleepover.

"I think we should order the white cheese pizza with spinach on it," suggested Beth.

"Monica and I like the pizza that has pepperoni on it with bits of pineapple," Melissa offered.

"Ewwww," exclaimed Sarah. "Well I can't have any pizza, I am a vegan." This statement caused Susan to roll her eyes at her sister and look away to avoid laughing.

"Wait, you are a what?" Beth squinted her eyes at her. "How come we are just finding this out? How come I never noticed?"

"What is a begin?" Little Monica asked as she scrunched up her face.

Melissa looked at Monica "Vee-gann… not begin. It is someone who doesn't eat meat or cheese."

"Or eggs." Sarah added with a nod.

Beth thought for a minute, "I will have to see what my aunt has for you then; she was planning on ordering pizza. Maybe they have a salad or something they can deliver with the pizza," Beth pondered, "hey, we always have lots of carrots around for the horses, you can munch on some carrots while we eat our yummy, hot, cheesily delicious pizza."

"Melissa…..," asked little Monica, "are chicken nuggets meat? I thought they were meat. If they are not meat what are they? I thought they were chicken but Sarah shared her nuggets with me at lunch and I ate them, but if Sarah doesn't eat meat and shared her food with me, does that make me a vee-gann too?"

Sarah grinned as all heads turned her way. She threw a fist in the air. "Got you all! Ha! I am just kidding. I want meat on my pizza, lots and lots of meat!"

Everyone then turned and looked at Susan. "Don't look at me, she pulls this joke all the time, ever since we had the vegan nanny taking care of us. Dad fired her when he caught her stealing his aquarium fish. She was taking them and letting them go in the lake in the park. He was wondering why they kept disappearing. He thought maybe his angel fish were eating each other ……."

Beth put up her hand and they all stopped. "I think we are being watched again." She stood up in her stirrups and twisted around to look behind them. They had entered the preserve and were following the edge of the trail which ran behind a

14

few small farmettes. These homes just had gardens and chickens; further up one of the little properties had goats with a couple of guardian dogs. Sophie must have smelled or heard the goats; she detested them and she stomped a hoof and angrily swished her tail back and forth as they stood there.

They looked around, but other than a white and purple striped curtain shifting in a bedroom window on the one house, there was nothing moving other than a few chickens scratching in the dirt and grass around a couple of sheds, one of which appeared to have been converted to a chicken coop. "Do you think someone was watching from that house?" asked Evelyn.

"I don't know, it is too far away; if their window is open, it may have been a breeze moving the curtain." Melissa said as she pushed her glasses up her nose. She had some orange haystring tied around the sides to prevent the glasses from falling off completely.

The girls waited a moment in silence. The only sound was faint clucking coming from the several contented chickens in the distance.

"I feel it too," Melissa said after a moment. "I do think maybe there was someone at the window."

Beth glanced at the girls. Evelyn was scanning the preserve around them; Sarah was squirming in her saddle. This was a long property and the house was sitting up at the far end; Susan was squinting and trying to see if she could spot anything up at the house. Monica was not really paying attention to the girls and took advantage of the halt to try braiding a section of Jahil's mane in front of the saddle.

Beth focused back on the house at the other end of the long yard. It was separated from the neighboring properties with a solid wood stockade fence, but the back of the property was open to the preserve and only separated by a woven wire field fence. She was sure they were being watched; it was the same creepy feeling that she had when she spotted the girl on the bicycle earlier and was made creepier by how quiet everything was. She could feel an uneasiness that pulled at the pit of her stomach and made the hairs on the back of her neck stand up. Then the silence was broken.

"I farted," said Sarah.

"Eww."

"You are gross."

"Why would you even tell us that?"

Monica began giggling uncontrollably.

"Thanks for sharing," Beth shook her head and looked up the trail.

"We have an hour until we need to get back. Sarah, move Sophie over to this side as we pass the goat farm up at the corner. Once we pass the goat farm, we will all have a little trot; stay behind me and nobody pass. We will trot down the ranger road through the field. I need everyone to stay on the road; don't go into the grass because there may be tortoise, gopher, or rabbit burrows out there. ON THE ROAD only," she emphasized.

This section of the preserve was called the 'Little Preserve' and was only about five hundred acres. Part of the little preserve had scattered orange trees as it had once been part of a large grove. This time of the year, the little oranges were shriveled up and dried and most had fallen to the ground. Other than the abandoned grove, the preserve here was mostly grassland with some areas of scrub bushes and saw palmettos. There were a few low spots and cypress marsh that would form ponds and small, shallow lakes during the rainy season.

They often saw hawks, deer, assorted snakes, wild turkeys, coyotes, bunnies, bald eagles and at this time of the year, the tall, gray sandhill cranes were raising their stilt-legged chicks. Beth had grown up riding these trails and she loved it out here. She would try to catalog the wildlife she would see on her many rides, but as much as she tried, Beth never saw any bobcats and she was beginning to think that the big alligator people claimed to have seen in the lake was a myth. Today they would not get to go to the lake because it was on the other side of the gate.

The gate at the end of the ranger road separated the little preserve from the middle section. The middle part of the reserve was part of a long-time cattle lease that the county had to honor when they set up the land preserve. Riders were allowed through and had to open and close the gate behind them, but Jayne wouldn't let the girls go through the cattle section without an adult because sometimes the cattle could get a bit aggressive. The big lake was in this cattle section and that is where other riders in the neighborhood would go to swim their horses.

"Beth," little Monica asked, "when will we get to swim with the horses?"

"Aunt Jayne said that once we are out of school for the summer, she would ride out here with us once or twice and let us swim in the big lake."

A big grin spread on Monica's face.

"Why does she have to come with us?" Sarah asked, "I like it better when we don't have grown ups with us."

"Because of Big Al in the lake. Jayne carries her pistol with her when we come in case she has to shoot Big Al."

Susan's mouth dropped open and she had a shocked look on her face, "Who is Al and why would Mrs. Jayne shoot him?"

Beth and Evelyn both laughed and Beth answered, "Al E. Gator is his name and he is a big 'gator. He usually lives in the big lake. I haven't seen him but other riders in the neighborhood have; someone said they saw him swimming around with a dead coyote in his mouth. They say he is more than ten feet long."

"And people still swim their horses in the lake?" Melissa had a shocked expression on her face.

"This is Florida, every lake probably has a gator or two in it. Besides, Jayne won't let us get off of our horses in the water. The gator won't come after a horse, horses are too big. But some of the other people do, they swim behind their horses or stand on the horses in the water and do backflips off of them and so far nobody has been attacked by Big Al….or any other gator in the lake."

The girls were momentarily quiet as they seemed to be deep in thought about the whole swimming in the lake idea. The horses picked their way down the path through the grass.

During the rainy season the path was firmer, and would sometimes get muddy spots, but they were still coming out of their dry season and now the path was deep sand which is why they kept the horses to a walk. The scattered orange trees had opened up to some grassland which was dotted with low growing saw palmetto and the occasional palm tree. Here and there were some oak trees with several of them showing damage from lightning strikes from the thunderstorms that rolled through almost daily during the summers.

The heat right now was strong, but at least it wasn't very humid….yet. Beth knew that over the next month or so, the heat would get more intense and that would start bringing in the rains and storms. She loved the summer and loved watching the daily drama that the skies offered every day.

Beth was lost in her thoughts as she led the girls further along. She was oblivious to their chatter. Her brain had moved on and was thinking about how she was going to be riding and working Gus almost every day once school was out. This was her last year to show Gus and she was determined to get to the Grand National Show in Oklahoma in the fall. She had shown Gus there many years ago when she was just a little older than Monica and she had done well enough to win ribbons in the class. Last year she was supposed to show Gus at Nationals again, but she had tripped going up the stairs her first week back at school and had broken her arm. She couldn't show, but she had gone with Aunt Jayne anyways to watch. Yes, this would be her year with Gus and she was determined to make it a great one.

Up ahead, Beth saw they were about to reach the ranger road that the park rangers drove their trucks and gas utility carts on.

The road would be firm for the horses as it was a hard-packed dirt and clay mix with a crushed shell and gravel type top on it. They were about to get to the ranger road for their trot when Beth noticed little Monica bouncing in her saddle with a panicked look on her face.

~ ~ ~

An hour later, they rode back up the driveway to Wildwood Stables. Jayne had finished setting up buckets for the horses' dinners and was sitting at her desk doing paperwork when she heard the gaggle of girls riding up towards the barn. From the sound of things, they had fun.

She stood in the hallway and watched them ride up the gravel driveway. The driveway ran between the big paddock on the left, and a row of smaller paddocks on the right. Jayne looked at the paddocks, the grass was dry and would soon start to get crispy. This was perhaps the driest April she had seen and the beginning of the rainy season was still at least a month away. She should probably look into having irrigation with sprinklers put in. She was going to have stalls added on the property and should ask the construction people about running sprinkler lines; she would add this note to her notebook so she wouldn't forget.

The girls rode up to the barn and Monica flung herself off Jahil and hopped up and down. "Mrs. Jayne, I had to go potty out on the trails and I need a bandage!"

"A bandage? Because you went potty?"

This was answered with eager nodding.

"I can explain," Beth grabbed Jahil's reins before the horse had a chance to walk off.

"Monica, come get Jahil and hold him. I will help you unsaddle in a minute, but you cannot just walk away from him." Beth scolded her.

As Monica took the reins and walked the little Arabian lesson horse to his stall, Beth continued, "we were on our way back in and were almost to the ranger road when she was hopping up and down in her saddle. She said she needed to pee and couldn't wait so we had her go behind a saw palmetto bush. When she squatted, she poked herself in the butt on a leaf and started crying."

"Oh dear, the poor thing. How badly did she get poked?'

Melissa who was Monica's neighbor and had baby sat her for the last couple of years chimed in, "she would only let me check. There isn't even a scratch, but I told her we would put a pretty bandage on it when we got back."

Jayne laughed, "That is not a problem. I have plenty of them around; she can take her pick on what one she wants."

Horses were cooled off and put away and Monica picked three bandages because she couldn't make up her mind - a cartoon one, a princess pink one and a camouflage pattered one (the later because she wanted to grow up to become like Beth… and camo would apparently play a factor in that).

The feed buckets were brought out and as Beth supervised the girls feeding, Jayne came through with a wheelbarrow full of hay. All of the horses were fed a flake of hay and then a flake was left right outside each stall for night feedings later on, all except for Gus, he was going out in the paddock overnight as usual.

…. Unfortunately, this night was going to be anything but usual.

# Chapter 3

It was a loud night. Jayne was happy for the house full of giggling and shrieking girls; it made her miss her husband less. His work was constantly sending him all over the world for one thing or another and while she was happy that he loved his work and got to travel, she disliked having a lonely house.

The girls were stuffed with pizza and they had baked a batch of chocolate chip cookies for desert while waiting for the pizza to be delivered. There was enough food left over for lunch tomorrow.

Jayne sat in a pool of light on the front porch steps of her house. She had her notebook and a pen in hand as she watched the girls all race around between the house and the barn playing tag with Cora the collie dog bouncing and running after them barking loudly and adding to the noise level. Cora knocked Monica down and without missing a beat, Monica popped up and kept chasing after Sarah but was soon distracted by a firefly.

A few more minutes of this and she would call them to settle down and throw hay to the horses for the night. Gus was trotting around the paddock tossing his head and flagging his tail. Beth had washed it after the trail ride and the rising moon made it look as if his nearly white mane and tail and legs were aglow. He was such a handsome pony. Gus was one of the few horses that was turned out overnight instead of going out during the day. With his big white blaze on his face, the pink skin on his nose sunburned and blistered easily, so night turnout worked best for him to protect him from the Florida sun.

Jayne was deep in thought and lowered her head to jot notes into her notebook about where she wanted to install sprinklers. A few moments later she realized the girls had gone quiet. She looked up.

They had stopped running around and Beth was walking towards the paddock. Gus had stopped and was staring down the long paddock towards the road. His head was up, his nostrils flared, and the snort he gave was a very loud blow that echoed through the still, night air. Beth opened the gate and walked across the paddock to her pony and rubbed his neck. She always gave him a scratch under his mane where he had an old scar. The injury had healed well but the scarred skin had made his hair grew back in a tiny white spot. Beth called it her 'good luck spot' and she scratched it for luck before each competition. "What do you see buddy?"

Down at the end of the driveway there was a glint of chrome. Beth watched as it flashed again and she realized it was a bicycle turning around and heading down the road. The girl was bicycling away rapidly, the white of the bicycle and the girl's white helmet picking up the light from the moon.

"Aunt, did you see?" Beth called, "she was watching us again and rode off on her bike."

"I saw." Jayne nodded.

Unfortunately, this stretch of rural road didn't have street lights so she was squinting to try to see the bicyclist better. "Girls, how about we get ready to head inside? Let's give the horses night hay and head for the house." Jayne looked at the

24

shadow furiously pedaling down the street, "I am going to walk the dog down to the gate and lock up. "

~ ~ ~

Jayne peeked into Beth's bedroom. The girls most certainly had a full and active day, they were all fast asleep and it wasn't even midnight. So much for their plans to sneak into the barn and give the horses the midnight snack of peppermint candies she had heard them discussing earlier.

Beth had her laptop computer open on her tummy so Jayne carefully stepped over the restful bodies in sleeping bags scattered around the floor. The room smelled of nail polish and there were hair accessories scattered about.

Beth had her dark blonde hair braided into two pigtail braids with big green bows on the ends, Sarah and Susan had also braided their coppery brunette hair. Susan had two braids with pastel pink bows and Sarah had one long braid with a black rubber band. Jayne smiled, of course Sarah the tomboy would not use bows. Melissa's short blonde hair just had tiny braids on the side of her face that were clipped up with gold barrettes and Evelyn's long blonde hair was put up in a bun. How was she going to sleep with a bun in her hair? Little Monica, who took the title of 'Pitchfork Princess' seriously, had fallen asleep wearing a crooked crystal tiara in her hair. Jayne stifled a laugh wondering what other hair accessories Monica had packed in her overnight bag.

Cora was resting next to Monica's sleeping bag and the collie thumped her tail. Apparently, the girls were not the only ones having a beauty treatment; Cora's nails were painted what looked like a glitter pink and she had a couple of sparkly hair clips fastened to the hair on the sides of her face and on the silky hair on her tail. Jayne looked around for her cat to see if he had been subject to similar treatment, but Bob seemed to have escaped the glittery clutches of the girls. He was probably hiding on a chair seat tucked under the dining room table.

Jayne quietly approached the bed and gingerly picked up the computer. Apparently, they had been looking at horses for sale. She closed the laptop with a faint click and placed it on the night table. She took a quick look around. Every electrical outlet had a cell phone plugged into it. She would need to make sure she didn't trip over the cords or step on anyone's phone. Exiting the room, she turned out the light and went to her own room.

~ ~ ~

The girls awakened to the smell of pancakes being cooked and they trudged out of the bedroom, sleepily stumbled down the hallway, and groaned as they walked into the living room where the early morning sun was streaming through the open curtains in the windows. They slumped into chairs around the kitchen table, except for Beth who opened the door to let the dog out, shut the door and then flopped onto the sofa and rolled over to hide her face from the sun. She mumbled something into the cushion.

"Beth, I didn't understand a thing you said." Jayne said as she put butter and syrup on the table.

"I said Evelyn and I found a horse online that she likes."

"When Evelyn's parents decide that they want to be in the market for a horse, they will let me know."

26

"They said they spoke to you about something, but they wouldn't tell me what," Evelyn announced. "I was hoping they were asking you to find a horse for my birthday in a few weeks."

Jayne paused. "Well….." she hesitated, then quickly added "they were asking about having a birthday party here for you so we were discussing that," Jayne picked her words carefully, "but there is no harm in looking and dreaming now is there?  Beth you need to come up to the table before Sarah takes all the pancakes or else you will be stuck with cold cereal."

Within minutes the chatter stopped and was replaced with clinking and scraping silverware sounds and one by one the girls finished and put their dishes into the sink and ran back to the bedroom to change clothes.

Jayne rinsed and loaded the plates into the dishwasher as the girls filed outside to feed the horses, but dropped a plate when she heard Beth's scream from outside.  As she raced to the front door, she was nearly trampled by Evelyn charging back into the house. "Gus is gone!"

Jayne grabbed her boots which were next to the front door and ran outside.  Beth had run across the paddock to where Jayne could see that the fence was down over by the tree in the road. Monica was sitting in the grass by the gate and was sobbing; Melissa was kneeling behind her rubbing her back and trying to comfort her.  Sarah and Susan were both standing behind Melissa and watching Beth in the distance.

Beth stood for several moments by the fence where the boards were laying on the ground, both hands were placed over her mouth trying to control her sobs.

"Girls, head over to the truck, let's take a drive and see if we can find him. Hopefully he just broke the fence and is just eating grass in a neighbor's yard." Jayne sat on the steps and pulled on her boots and then disappeared in the house for a moment and then reappeared with her keys and purse.

She headed to the paddock to grab the halter and lead rope from the hook by the gate, but the hook was empty. Beth must have it, she concluded. She headed to the big farm truck and everyone piled in. When they reached the end of the driveway, Evelyn hopped out and unlocked the gate, then locked it behind them as the truck drove out. She walked up to Beth and put her arms around her. "Mrs. Jayne says we are going to search the neighborhood. He may just be eating grass somewhere."

Beth shook her head and still with a hand over her mouth, stumbled to the truck. "He isn't the one that broke the fence," she mumbled through her sobs, "someone took him. Someone has my Gussie."

# Chapter 4

Jayne turned off the ignition in the truck. Beth was looking at the fence but couldn't get any more words out. "Beth, do you have his halter and leadrope?"

No more words, just her head shaking back and forth to indicate a 'no' as tears streamed down her face.

They all exited the truck. The girls ran up to the fence and were looking around. "Don't touch anything," instructed Melissa right as Susan was reaching down to pick up a board, "there might be clues or fingerprints."

Melissa leaned down to look at the board and pushed her glasses back up her nose. "Mrs. Jayne, someone hammered these boards out."

Jayne was inspecting the boards. There were most definitely round, dented hammer marks on the boards where it appeared someone had hit them to loosen the nails out of the post, and the middle board had even cracked at the end. "Beth, you said you don't have his halter?"

"No," Beth said as she struggled to compose herself, "it wasn't hanging on the fence. I thought maybe you had already brought him into the barn before cooking breakfast, but then I looked down to the tree by the road and saw the fence was down. That is when I knew he was stolen."

"Let's take a quick drive through the neighborhood," Jayne frowned; she had a sick feeling in her stomach but she had to remain calm and think. "It does appear that someone took him.

We don't know when this happened, maybe whoever took him is still leading or riding him."

"Unless they brought a trailer and loaded him in. He could be anywhere!" added Sarah.

Jayne shot Sarah a look to quiet her down as this just made Beth sob again which then made Monica cry. That thought had occurred to her also, but she didn't want to alarm the girls. If the thief had used a trailer, he really could be anywhere, but Gus wasn't overly fond of horse trailers.

"Well, the more I think of it… I don't think that would be likely. If someone did try to put Gus in a trailer, they probably would have given up. You know how bad he can be when he doesn't want to load." Jayne said.

Beth gave a sob that was half muffled laugh. "Yeah, they would have given up on him if they were trying to load him."

~ ~ ~

Several minutes later they were all back at the barn. A drive through the roads in the neighborhood didn't reveal anyone leading or riding Gus anywhere and Jayne had pulled out her cellphone and called the police department as they headed back to Wildwood Stables.

"Girls, let's get the horses fed while we wait for the Detective to come. I am sure they are hungry and not happy that their breakfast is late."

They reached the farm and the girls had started feeding, but Beth was not to be seen. Jayne looked down the barn aisle and saw Beth who sat slumped on the bench behind the barn by the wooden round pen fence. Jayne started towards her, but then stopped. When Beth was ready, she would come into the barn again. Beth's emotions had always been complicated and Jayne knew that often it was best to let her compose herself before intruding. Beth had a habit of pushing people away when she was upset and emotional. Yes, when Beth was ready to talk, she would know.

~ ~ ~

All of the horses were busy munching their late breakfast as Detective Herrero pulled up in his unmarked cruiser. "Girls, stay here for a bit while I talk to the Detective."

"I will water horses," Susan volunteered.

"Sarah and I will rake the hallway," Evelyn grabbed Sarah by the back collar of her shirt and drug her to the equipment room where the rakes hung.

Melissa just shrugged "I'll sweep the tack room or something."

Jayne looked for Monica and saw that she had joined Beth and was sitting on her lap over on the bench. Her little arms were thrown around Beth's neck and both faces were turned away from her.

Jayne walked Detective Herrero around the farm and showed him the fence that had been hammered out of the posts. He examined the wood and showed Jayne that there were also pry marks from the claw of the hammer. Unfortunately, he told them that there wasn't a good way to get fingerprints off rough cut wood.

Jayne pulled out her phone and sent some photos of Gus to the Detective's email along with the description of the missing pony.   He would notify the Agricultural officers that monitored all horses coming into and out of the state and would have the local Agricultural officers notify all boarding barns in the area in case someone stole him and tried boarding him at another stable.

They exchanged business cards and Jayne headed back into the barn.  The girls were all sitting in the chairs outside of the barn office and they were all bent down looking and tapping on their phones.  "I don't want you posting anything online just yet.  Let me decide what we want to say and then you can share what I post, OK?"  All of the phones disappeared back into pockets.

"Detective Herrero does think Gus was stolen.  He thinks whoever did it jumped the fence and got the halter then put it on him, walked Gus to the tree and then took the fence down and stepped over the bottom fence board.  We do not know if Gus was led off, ridden off in the halter or loaded into a trailer...."  she put her hand up when the girls looked like they were going to comment .... "I did tell him that he doesn't load for just anyone and that we have doubts about that theory," she sighed, "but we cannot rule anything out."

The next few hours were spent with Jayne and Beth fixing the broken fence after which horses were put out for the day and Jayne helped the girls clean stalls.   On Sundays, she sometimes didn't ride any of the training horses and only gave light workouts from the ground using her long-lines or a lunge rope, and today she only had two group lessons after lunch. She called those students and rescheduled them and made her apologies.  She checked the time; her husband had flown to Belgium to make a presentation to some big manufacturing company, but today he would be spending the day in England. Whenever he had to travel to Europe on business, he always tried to spend a day in London visiting his mother. Tomorrow he would fly from London to New York and then home to Florida. She quickly sent him a message to call whenever he got a chance.

Halfway through cleaning stalls, they broke for lunch. Jayne watched the girls eating their pizza in the barn office. Susan had heated hers in the microwave, but everyone else was eating theirs cold, except Beth who just stared at her plate. "Do you think he is somewhere close by?' Beth finally asked.

Jayne went over and sat next to her and put her arm around her niece. "Possibly. But there are about 20 bigger farms in this neighborhood and about 100 little farmettes and who knows how many of those farmettes have horses in the backyards. The police are trying to go door to door to ask neighbors. Maybe someone has a security camera that caught something, or maybe someone was out late at night or very early in the morning and saw Gus. Let's give them a little time to work and report back to us."

Beth was still deep in thought and was chewing on her lower lip. Jayne knew that look. Beth had an idea. "Does Uncle Matt still have that drone he got for his birthday last year? We could check all the farms out from the air."

For the first time since breakfast, Jayne smiled. "He sure does!" She jumped out of her seat and jogged towards the house. "Beth, you are brilliant!"

# Chapter 5

"Nothing, absolutely nothing," Beth wailed as she handed the drone controls to Jayne. This started Monica sniffling again as she turned her head towards Melissa and hugged her around her waist. Susan walked over and stroked Monica's long dark hair. Sarah and Evelyn hugged Beth.

"Let me fly this thing home before the charge runs out. Girls, if anyone feels like riding, you can hop on the horses bareback today. I am sure they would just love to stretch their legs a little bit."

"I don't feel like going," Beth whispered as she watched Jayne land the drone. It bounced sideways a couple of times and then flipped over in the grass. Monica unwound her arms from Melissa's waist and skipped over to pick the drone up.

Jayne put her arms around Beth. "I know dear. Why don't you go brush Dallas for a while? Maybe it will help to distract you a little bit." She could feel Beth shake her head side to side then turn her face to wipe her nose on her sleeve.

"I am so glad you did not snot up the front of my shirt. It is bad enough when the horses do that; it is one thing to go around wearing horse snot, it is another thing to be wearing niece snot."

Beth chuckled for about a half second, "I just want to lie down for a little bit."

Beth broke out of the hug and walked towards the barn. Jayne watched her go into the barn office and she knew Beth would lie on the over-stuffed leather sofa in there.

"Are you girls going to go ride bareback for a little?" Jayne inquired. None of the girls looked overly excited. "You can ride in the arena for a little bit and I will keep an eye on you while I work on my notes."

"Mrs. Jayne," Melissa asked, "can we ride down the road to the corner and back too? "Monica was hopping up and down, apparently she liked that idea..

"The little Mexican jumping bean here, has to ride double with someone," Jayne started.

"I'm not Mexican! I'm Cuban." protested Monica as she stopped jumping and crossed her arms in front of her.

Hmmm…. Jayne made a mental note to explain what Mexican jumping beans are, but that would have to be later. "So, as I was saying, I want you girls to take turns bareback in the arena with Monica riding double behind someone. No cantering with her, she can just walk and trot. When you go down the road I want her behind Evelyn for the trip."

After spending about 30 minutes of supervised riding bareback in the arena, they organized in the middle to let the horses rest a moment and to decide who was riding which horse down the road. Jayne thought it looked like a meeting so she put her notebook down on the chair and walked into the office to grab a drink out of the refrigerator. Beth was still sound asleep on the sofa with an arm lying over her eyes. Jayne left her there without disturbing her; she would awaken Beth when her parents came to pick her up.

~ ~ ~

Beth heard her aunt come into the office and open the refrigerator for a drink, but she didn't stir. She kept her eyes closed with her arm thrown over them. Would they find her pony, her dear and beloved pony who was her best friend? She grew up riding Gus; she learned to jump obstacles on Gus; she was hoping to one day teach her little sister to ride on him, when she was old enough, so that her sister would grow up with the wonderful experience of loving and riding and sharing secrets with a pony. She had hoped that her little sister would also get to show Gus at horse shows and win ribbons and jump and have all kinds of fun and happy memories.

She felt a tear trickle down her cheek. As of now, Beth's future happiness had been taken from her. Gus was the best friend for Beth to tell her secrets to and to share her problems with. He would never tell another soul and he never passed judgement on her or told her what to do; he just listened and that always made her feel better. He was her best friend and he was gone. She had to get him back.

Flyers. They would have to put flyers all over the neighborhood. She would be going home to her parents for the week and she would have to ask her aunt to hang them at every corner. Somewhere, Gus was being hidden on someone's farm. With his coloring, he should be easy to find; at some point, whoever had him would pull him out of a barn or wherever he was being hidden and someone would see the orange-red pony with the almost white mane and tail…. right?

~ ~ ~

"Listen up," commanded Evelyn from huddle of horses they had made in the arena. "Melissa and I think we should see if we can find any clues when we go down the road."

"Maybe the thief rode Gus away and dropped the hammer. I would think it would be hard to ride a strange horse in a halter and leadrope with no bridle, AND carry a hammer at the same time." Melissa pondered.

"I could do it." Sarah boasted.

"Only until you fart on the horse's back and it spooks. You would drop the hammer then," her sister teased.

"Nuh-uh …..get me a hammer; I'll do it now and show you…..maybe if I was on Sophie she would spook if I farted, but I am on Jahil and he won't." Monica gave her a sideways look and a pout from her spot behind Evelyn. She was upset that she couldn't ride Jahil bareback on her own.

"Don't be silly, Sarah," Melissa changed the subject, "wouldn't it be great if the thief DID drop the hammer? The police can't get fingerprints on fence board, but they could on a hammer. The TV detectives do all the time." She paused to think for a moment about how they did things on the TV detective shows, "but if we find the hammer, we can't pick it up unless we have gloves or something like that."

"I have my riding gloves in my grooming box. I can pick it up and then show you that I can ride and carry the hammer." Sarah turned the horse and started riding out of the arena and trotted up to the barn where she hopped down from Jahil and disappeared inside.

"She is determined to ride and carry a hammer. She will not stop until she does it and shows you all." Susan warned them.

"Jahil is trained for Western and neck reins. Anyone can ride him one handed and carry something in the other hand." Evelyn pointed out.

"Don't remind her of that or else she will want to trade horses out on the street to show you she can do it." Susan begged.

Sarah appeared with Jahil and mounted from the mounting steps in front of the barn. She trotted over with her riding gloves on her hands. "Let's go, these will make my hands sweat so I want to hurry and find the hammer and ride back with it."

"There might not be a hammer." Susan pointed out.

"But we need to find clues. With clues, we can solve this and find Gus and get the thief arrested." Sarah turned Jahil to go out of the arena again. "The Pitchfork Princesses have a mystery to solve."

"For Gus. Let's get him back." Melissa said with grim conviction.

"Let's get him back," repeated Evelyn, "for Beth."

"We can be the Pitchfork Princess Detective agency!" Susan joked.

And on that note, they exited the arena and found Mrs. Jayne to tell her they were headed out.

"Just to the corner and back, and only walking," instructed Jayne. "I will be watching from the feed shed."

Jayne watched the girls head down the driveway, single file as she dragged a chair from the arena's spectator area over to the front of the feed shed. She set out the little buckets and the bags of grain and the tubs of supplements and started putting together the evening's dinner for the horses. She opened the bag of peppermints that the girls didn't feed at midnight. Each horse got two of the peppermints in their bucket.

Each bucket had a horse name on it and they were color coded.... the horses that needed special Senior feed had red buckets, the horses needing the low carb and high fat feed had yellow buckets, the horses on the regular feed had green buckets. The white board on the open door of the shed listed the amounts for each horse and which supplements to add to the buckets. Jayne liked being organized, it made things easier.

She paused to watch the girls. They had stopped partway down the road where the little 2-acre farmette with the cute blue house was for sale. They were looking at something underneath Magic who was being ridden double by Evelyn and Monica. She saw Sarah dismount and pick something up, and then she walked over and appeared to be talking to someone that Jayne couldn't see.

Jayne leaned down and realized she had forgotten the thyroid medicine for Kammy's food bucket, so she went into the feed shed, located the plastic jar and sat down outside the shed again. Looking back down the street, she watched Sarah walk Jahil to the corner of the property and then stand on a fence rail to hop back up on Jahil's back. The group continued up the road and Jayne saw a brightly clad woman headed back up that property's driveway. It was the real estate agent; so apparently, Ms. Miller was showing the house today. The group continued up the road.

Because Mr. Jacobs had passed away, the blue house sat vacant while it was for sale and kids in the neighborhood would meet back there at night to do who knows what. Ms. Miller was constantly having to fix things up when she was showing the house to a potential buyer. Jayne hoped the house would sell quickly. She would see about asking Detective Herrero if there was anything to be done in the meantime because she didn't like the idea of people she didn't know doing things she didn't know about so closely to her home and her farm.

Jayne had a thought…were the trespassing kids stealing things and meeting there? Could they have decided to go for a joy ride on Gus and they left him behind the house? The Jacobs' property didn't have a barn, just an old chicken coop, and his rickety fence would not have been able to hold a horse. No, she thought. If some little lawbreaker was trying to hide Gus practically across the street, he would have found a way to get home for his breakfast.

Jayne looked down and started gathering the set-up dinners and then she realized that without thinking, she had set up dinner for Gus. A tear trickled down her face and she quickly wiped it away. No tears now. Later, when everyone was gone she would let herself cry. Not now. She didn't want the girls, especially Beth to sense the hopelessness she felt.

# Chapter 6

The late afternoon sun was making the lake shimmer and a very slight breeze had kicked up, making the Spanish moss in the oak trees gently lift and sway in the breeze. Evelyn decided that they would walk to the corner on the south shoulder of the road, and they would return down the north shoulder of the road so that they could check both sides. Evelyn walked up to a low branch and carefully pulled some moss down and stretched forward to offer it to Magic as a snack.

The lake was directly across the street from the stable and there were only a few properties on their small road. On the south side of the road, there was a spit of land on the lake, Old Mr. Jacob's property which was for sale, and then a little farmette at the corner. On the north side of the road were three smaller 5 and 8 acre farms and then the bigger 15-acre property of Wildwood Stables.

Evelyn steered the group back to the road and they were on their way, Magic happily munching the long strand of moss. The girls scoured the side of the road. "What are we looking for again?" asked little Monica.

"Anything that looks like it shouldn't be here," answered Evelyn.

"Like what kind of anything?"

"Anything, anything," groaned Susan.

"But especially a hammer," added her sister.

"So, we need to look for an anything?" Monica scratched her chin under the strap of her riding helmet and then began scanning the grass and the edge of the roadway.

They were approaching the house that was for sale. Up by the garage, they saw a lady carrying bottles and cans out from behind the house and stuffing them in the garbage can. The lady had big and poofy blonde hair and was dressed in a tight, tailored double breasted pink jacket and a tight, black skirt. Her tall, black stiletto heels kept getting stuck in the grass as she struggled with two small boxes she now carried to the trash.

"I think that is the lady whose picture is on the for- sale sign," observed Melissa as she pushed her glasses back up her nose. She had tied a haystring onto her glasses so they wouldn't fall off while she was riding or cleaning stalls.

The realtor started her trek down the gravel driveway pulling the wheeled garbage can behind her. The girls paused and watched in fascination as the pink lady's high-heeled shoes made her ankles wobble and wiggle all the way down the rocky, gravel driveway.

"I'll bet you ten bucks she falls."

"Sarah, you don't have ten bucks," claimed her sister. "Her shoes are pretty; I hope she doesn't break them on the gravel. Remember when mom ruined her nice heels on the cobblestones when we were on vacation in Florence?"

"You have been to Italy? Evelyn asked.

"Well duh….. our dad is from there and we visit our grandparents."

Evelyn started the group moving again and took about three steps when Jahil who was being ridden next to them stepped on something crunchy in the grass and took a little hop forward, stepped on his own hoof and then tripped.

"What was that?" Sarah asked as she quickly took up her reins to stop Jahil.

Evelyn looked down at something beige in the grass. "I don't know."

"Whatever it was," Melissa said from behind the two, "it squirted something onto Magic's back leg. It looks like oil.

"It's a hammer!" shrieked Monica and her little butt started bouncing up and down behind Evelyn.

Evelyn shortened up her reins on Magic, expecting him to react to the child bouncing on his back, but he was a good boy and stood still.

"Hammers don't squirt oil, silly," Susan said as she rolled her eyes.

"Then maybe it is an anything." Monica gave a satisfied grin when Susan opened her mouth to argue with her and then changed her mind.

The girls all looked at Magic's right hind leg. He was a black horse with a miniscule white dot on his forehead and both hind legs had short white socks for markings. The white hair of his right hind sock now had a line of black liquid dripping down onto his pale hoof.

"You are going to have to wash that off when we get back." Sarah hopped off and picked up the beige plastic bottle that was squashed where Jahil had stepped on it. She pulled off some hair and grass that was clinging to the sticky bottle and carefully turned the dripping bottle with a green cap over to look for a label. The label was missing.

The rickety rumble of the garbage can wheels was almost upon them. "You girls!" the pink lady waved at them as she hurried at what seemed to be an impossibly speedy wobble towards them. Sarah sucked her lips in to stifle a giggle and her freckled nose quivered as her nostrils flared. Behind her she heard Melissa quietly snort a laugh. "Do you know who in the neighborhood hangs out here on this property?"

The girls all looked at each other. "What do you mean?" asked Evelyn, "we don't live in this neighborhood, we just ride at the barn down at the end." She pointed towards the Wildwood property.

The pink lady set the garbage can at the end of the driveway and carefully poked her way through the grass towards the mounted girls.

"Every time I show this house, I have to come over and clean up behind it. I keep finding cans and bottles and cigarettes. I have someone coming in twenty minutes and I am so glad that I got here early after the mess on the driveway today."

The girls looked at the gravel on the drive. Nothing looked unusual.

"I got here and someone had spilled black paint, right here where anyone coming in would see it." She waved her hands with her pink fingernails in the general direction of the driveway. "It is a good thing old Mr. Jacobs left a garage full of gardening tools behind when he passed on. I was able to rake the rocks around so the paint wouldn't show."

Melissa could faintly make out a few scattered black rocks among the white and gray.

"Maybe it was this?" Sarah showed her the plastic bottle. "My horse stepped on it and it squirted black stuff on that horse's leg." She pointed at Magic.

The pink lady gingerly took the dripping bottle from Sarah. "Damn garbage," she quickly put her other hand over her mouth. "I am sorry I said 'damn' girls." She then opened up the lid on the garbage can and tossed it in.

"Don't worry about it, you should hear what comes out of my dad's mouth when he burns food at the restaurant." Sarah grinned. "It is a lot worse."

Susan wouldn't let an opportunity go to get business for her dad. "He owns DelRizzo's, you should go eat there," she nodded. "Fine Italian dining," she added.

The pink lady smiled. "Thank you, I will make a note of that."

Sarah rolled her eyes at her sister and led Jahil forward a few feet where the fence started and she climbed up onto the middle rail and hopped up on Jahil's back.

The pink lady's bosom rang and she stuck her hand down the front of her jacket to pull a pink cell phone out of her bra. Turning away from the girls, she picked and waddled and wiggled her way back up the driveway as she gave directions to whoever was on the phone with her.

"Sarah, what if the bottle was a clue? You just handed it over and it is in the garbage now." Melissa pointed out.

"You heard Wobble Lady; it is garbage and she finds garbage here every time. There isn't anything special about that bottle. Now let's keep going, I have a hammer to find."

~ ~ ~

On their way back, Monica, who liked shiny stuff, spied something glinting on the other side of the road, almost where they had found the plastic bottle.

"Is it a clue?" Susan excitedly asked.

"I hope it is the hammer!" Sarah waited for a car to slowly roll by and up into the driveway before she crossed the street to check.

"We were already over there; if there was a hammer there, how did we miss it?" Susan wondered loudly.

"Maybe it is an 'anything'." Monica slanted her eyes and grinned at Susan, but Susan didn't pay attention as she focused her attention on what her twin was making a beeline for.

Everyone held their breath as Sarah hopped down and picked the object up out of the grass. It was a horse shoe. She held it up for everyone to see.

"We did it! A clue! Now we know the thief didn't use a trailer and Gus was walked away." Sarah mounted from the fence again and headed back across the street to rejoin the others. That is when they heard it.

Click, clop, clop, clop; click, clop, clop, clop....as Jahil walked across the asphalt roadway. Jahil was supposed to have two shoes on his front feet and barefoot behind. There should have been two clicks and two clops for every stride. Evelyn pointed down at Jahil's front hooves.

"That is Jahil's shoe. He must have stepped on it and loosened it when he tripped after stepping on the bottle, then it came off after a few more steps."

Melissa let out a sad sigh, "So it is not a clue."

"Why couldn't it have been a hammer? We need to find a hammmmmeeerrrrr," lamented Sarah.

Several minutes later, the sad little group made their way home. There was no hammer. They had inspected every bush and fence along the way because Melissa remembered that in the movies the searchers always found hair or torn clothing on something and that would be a clue, but there wasn't any white tail hair from the missing pony and there were not any shreds of clothing to be seen. The grass on the side of the road wouldn't show any footprints.

"This detective stuff is harder than it seems on TV." Melissa gave an exasperated sigh. "We don't have any more information than we did before."

"No hammer, …..but I did prove that I could ride back holding a horse shoe. That has to count for something."

# Chapter 7

"Shampoo and just trim the ends a bit please, Karen." Jayne settled into the chair of Karen Green who lived around the corner. Karen had been cutting hair in her home for most of the neighborhood for the last year, ever since losing her husband. It was a meager living, but it was how she brought in extra money for herself and her daughter.

"I see a few more gray hairs cropping up Jayne," Karen said, as her fingers ran through the chestnut brown hair and picked at the gray hairs by Jayne's ears, "are you sure you don't want them colored? I got some new products in this week, you know."

"Hey, I have earned every single one of these gray hairs, leave them alone!" Jayne laughed and swatted at her hand, "and I have earned a bunch of gray hairs this past weekend."

"You and me both." Karen put a plastic cape around Jayne's neck and tilted the chair back over the sink. "Did I ever tell you that Caitlyn's dad had always promised her a horse?" she paused, "When Jeremy was alive and we had more money…well, he was always promising her a horse, you know. He grew up with a pony with a black tail and used to tell Caitlyn stories of his Champ. Oh, did I tell you that she used to take lessons over at Foxhill Farms over on Aristides Lane and she always dreamed of having a horse like Champ? She would ride her bike over there for her lessons when we had the money to pay for them."

"Yes, I remember you telling me two or three visits ago that she used to take lessons, but that is so sad about her dad," Jayne paused, it is good that she has happy memories of her father."

"I hope you are not offended that Caitlyn was riding at Foxhill. No offense, I am sure you are a great instructor, but Caitlyn had a friend from school who rides there, you know. If not for that Jeremy would have had her ride with you since you are a little bit closer."

"No worries," Jayne assured her.

Karen began to wet Jayne's hair with warm water. "Is this too cold or too hot for you?"

"Perfect" Jayne mumbled. She really didn't want to talk, she had too much on her mind. She had a folder full of flyers she was going to staple on the wooden telephone and light poles around the neighborhood after her hair appointment.

"Well, Caitlyn had to stop riding when Jeremy had his accident, you know, but she really missed riding and the horses. Then Jeremy was gone." Karen choked back a sob as she poured shampoo into her hand and started lathering Jayne's hair. "Caitlyn misses her dad so much. She has been able to do a bit of riding here and there working over at Foxhill. She rides her bike over there after school and on weekends; she feeds, brings horses in and cleans up the horses' cages in the little barn behind the big barn."

Jayne crinkled her forehead. Cages? She must mean stalls. The shampoo massage on her head and the warm water felt good. She could just fall asleep at any second. She had tossed and turned all night long so it would be so easy to just close her eyes right now. It was so peaceful …. until Karen Green continued.

"She kept bugging me that she wanted a horse, and our property is fenced and big enough. So, last week she just got me on a day where I was feeling sad, you know, and she asked me if I would let her have a horse if she could pay for it. I felt safe saying yes. We don't have the money for that, you know.. Everyone tells me they are expensive."

"Mmmmhhh," Jayne mumbled, "yes, I know."

"Well, I thought she was just working for free rides, you know." She started to rinse the shampoo, "but all along, they were paying her a little bit here and a little bit there."

Jayne opened her eyes and turned her head. "Oh, Karen …..don't tell me…..she saved up enough to buy a horse?!?!? Your daughter bought a horse?!?!"

"Oh, no no no," Karen laughed, "it is worse than that." She wrung out Jayne's hair. "Someone GAVE her a horse."

"You have got to be kidding me."

"No! Really. I woke up yesterday and went out to feed the chickens and collect eggs from the coop and there was a horse in our back yard. I was very surprised!"

Jayne held her breath. "Yesterday morning …..Sunday?"

"Yes! There he was! Just running, and snortin' you know. I don't know the first thing about horses and …Ow, that hurts!"

Jayne looked down at her hand. She hadn't realized she had grabbed Karen by the wrist, so she let her go. "Does this horse have four white socks, a white blaze and white mane and tail?"

"N-no," she said as she rubbed her wrist. "I mean no, he has a black mane and tail…..I think he has white feet but I don't remember how many. Are you OK?"

Jayne let her breath out. She didn't realize she had been holding it. She sank back down in the chair. "He sounds lovely."

"Oh, he is!" she paused. "I think it is a he….. yes, now I remember. Caitlyn said she named him Champ, just like her daddy's horse. That sounds like a boy's name to me, you know." Karen started combing through Jayne's wet hair. "She said someone at Foxhill was giving him away. I had to drive her to that Hay Depot place so she could buy him some food with the money she works for and she had some leftover money so we went to the Fox and Hound for some supplies afterwards. "

She stopped combing and started scissoring Jayne's hair and clipping up sections with lime green and purple hair clips as she worked from section to section. "I don't know whether to be proud of her, or mad at her. We could use that money for other things, you know."

"I completely understand. But horses tend to keep a lot of kids out of trouble. The kids keep busy and have to be responsible. I know a lot of parents that use the horses or riding lessons as a way to make the kids keep their grades up. Maybe you should try that; if she works all the time, her grades may suffer. Tell her the horse stays if the grades stay up. It will make her manage her time better. There may be some good of this after all."

Karen waved out the window to someone and hollered "Come on in Tonya." She started pulling clips out of Jayne's hair and plopped the scissors and comb into the jar of blue liquid. She opened the top drawer and rummaged around to look for the brush she wanted. "I like that idea. You know, you may be right. It may bring about some good."

The screen door at the front of the house banged closed and Jayne waved at Tonya Miller as she strode in. She was wearing yellow stiletto heels that clicked across the tile floor, and a short sundress with yellow and pink flowers. She had a pink scarf around her head covering her hair and she pulled off her sunglasses. "Hello Jayne, I met some of your riders yesterday." She didn't wait for Jayne to reply, "Karen you have to help me. I was showing Mr. Jacobs' house last evening and was picking up garbage. I got something on my hands and didn't notice but it got all over my phone and then I put my phone up to my head to talk and it got in my hair." She took the scarf off and her bright blonde hair had a big black splotch right by her ear.

"My potential buyer saw it and told me; I was so embarrassed." She stopped to fan herself with her hand.

Karen had just picked up the hairdryer, but put it down and walked towards Tonya. She ran her fingers through the blonde locks.

"Help me Karen, I tried everything last night to take it out. I don't know what it is; I kept shampooing and I tried putting mayonnaise on it, but nothing is getting it out. I can't cut it out; that will take a big chunk of hair off," she wailed, "do you have something that can take it out?"

"You were picking up garbage at old Mr. Jacob's place," Jayne pointed out, "it was probably a bottle of hair dye. That old man always had black, black hair. He was always chasing after the old widowed ladies at his church…..and some of the younger ones too, come to think of it." Jayne laughed.

"Oh, he didn't do his own hair, I dyed it for him here. He wouldn't have had any at his house, you know."

Jayne grinned, "It wouldn't surprise me if he was touching up his own roots at home."

Karen and Tonya both nodded agreement. "Let me give Jayne a blow dry and I will see what we can do."

Tonya sat down in the chair Karen offered and reached over to pick up a brochure. In the process of doing so, the rickety table rocked sideways and several of the bottles displayed on the table top wiggled and fell off. Toyna bent down and picked them up. The assorted bottles, were beige with green tops and had pretty green and brown patterned labels. "Karen, honey; what are these?"

"Oh, let me help you with that, that is new stock I started using and I liked it so much I just started carrying the whole line of products for sale. They are botanical based, you know. There is a shampoo, conditioner, a pump hair spray and some coloring products …..oh, and a detangler that I just love, love, love….Jayne, I am going to give your hair a few squirts of the detangler, let me know how you like it."

"The bottle of hair dye I picked up at Mr. Jacobs' place was beige like this but didn't have a label on it."

"Oh, I didn't carry this product when Mr. Jacobs was alive, so I doubt that one of my bottles ended up over there." She turned on the hairdryer and picked up her vented brush and went back to work on Jayne's hair.

# Chapter 8

There were no leads as to what happened with Gus. Not one single lead.

Jayne handed the telephone back to her husband without looking at him; she just stared straight ahead at the TV without really looking at it. He took the phone, hung up the call and put the phone on the coffee table. He then picked up the TV remote and pushed the mute button. "So, what did the police say?"

Tears welled up in Jayne's eyes and Matt used his thumb to catch the one closest to him and wipe it away.

"He says they went door to door around the neighborhood. Nobody saw anything Saturday night or Sunday morning. There are two people with new horses in the neighborhood, but one is the Green's bay horse and the other is an appaloosa. Nobody in the neighborhood has a red pony with a whiteish mane and tail."

She paused to breathe deeply then continued, "they reviewed security cameras but nobody with a camera lived close enough to the road to show anything, but they did check records at the Ag Station for people leaving Florida and there were seven flaxen chestnuts with four white socks and a blaze that left Florida Sunday and Monday. The Ag station copies the paperwork for the horses leaving or entering the state and they copy the drivers' licenses and get the vehicles' license plates. They are going to follow up on those leads. They also sent photos of Gus to the Ag officers at the station so if they do see Gus leave they can stop the hauler."

"Sugar, would a person be able to get a Coggins paper that quickly?"

"They could get a health certificate that quickly from a vet, but for a Coggins….no, we usually have to wait a couple of weeks. The vet has to send bloodwork to a state approved lab to run the test. I have expedited paperwork before, but still, that couldn't be turned around this quickly."

"Can someone counterfeit or alter the papers to match the horse?"

Jayne thought for a moment, "possibly, but I would think the Ag officers at the station would be able to catch fake paperwork, if not when presented, then if they double check against the official copy on file with the Ag Department."

"Darling, that is a good thing, there is still hope that he will be found."

"You don't understand." Jayne shook her head, "I just feel that he is nearby and the police are too focused on a theory that he was hauled away somewhere. I don't think he was put in a trailer. You remember when we went to pick him up as a surprise for Beth. It took three hours to get him in the horse trailer to bring him here."

Matt scratched his head and yawned. He was still suffering jet lag from the time difference. "But he has been so much better at loading since then. It only took 15 minutes last time."

"Yes, for me or for Beth. But he wouldn't load for just anyone without making them give up and go steal an easier horse. If the thief was parked on the road with a trailer, we would have seen evidence of them trying to load Gussie. It didn't occur to me when I was speaking to Detective Herrero, but we would have seen the grass torn up from Gus trying to avoid going in. If they were on the pavement, we would have seen scrapes on the pavement from his horse shoes. If he did go in, we would have seen a pile of manure…. horses almost always poop before they go in a trailer." She paused, "and think about it, if someone pulled onto our road with a horse trailer, where would they have turned the trailer around? They couldn't pull up our driveway at night because of the gate; they would have to be magicians to turn it around in front of the lake ….. try backing and driving around all of those trees in the dark! …. And we are nearly a half-mile from the corner. I doubt anyone would have backed the trailer down the road for a half-mile."

"You are right. There is no way Gus willingly went into a strange trailer for a person he didn't know." Matt pulled Jayne into a hug. "Your hair smells good."

"I visited Karen today. She used this new spray detangler in my hair and I liked it so I bought a bottle of it."

"It smells like sunflowers; it is nice." He took another whiff. "I am so knackered, I don't think I can keep my eyes open another minute. I am headed to bed." Jayne smiled. Despite living in the United States for 20 years, he still had his British accent and phrases and it was always more evident when he was sleepy.

"I'll be there shortly. I have some laundry to throw in the dryer and I think I am going to just start jotting things down as I think of them or remember them. There has to be something that will lead us to him." She leaned her head on the back of the sofa and put both hands on her head. She felt the sofa cushions rise as Matt stood up. "I also need to put some carefully worded posts out on social media and that Missing Horse internet page. Someone, somewhere knows where he is and I hope with all my being that they will do the right thing."

Jayne put her hands down and opened her eyes. Matt was standing over her. He leaned down and pressed a kiss to her forehead. "We will find him."

~ ~ ~

Jayne isn't sure how she got through the week. Bunny and Charlie were the married couple that lived on the farm in a little cottage. They worked for her on the weekdays and did their best to keep her on track. Charlie was picking stalls with his customary efficiency; Bunny, who knew the schedule well, pulled out the appropriate horses and had them groomed, saddled and ready for Jayne to hop on and exercise them. One after another, Jayne rode. They were mostly Morgan horses and one leggy 3 year- old Friesian stallion and a couple of tall Saddlebred horses that someone had brought to her to prepare for an upcoming show where they were hoping to sell the horses. They were all being trained and conditioned for various show events.

The Friesian was still young and Jayne was hoping he would make a saddle seat horse but that was still debatable; he still had some growing to do so she kept his workouts light and short and she concentrated on teaching him to soften his mouth and give to the bit without being heavy in the bridle and also worked on making him a little more responsive to leg.

The one saddlebred was being worked as a Western pleasure show horse and she focused on making him better with his neck reining, which would make him steer with just the feel of the rein touching his neck. This horse really had a good mouth and carried himself well, but he was stiff through his body, so Jayne worked on making his body a little more supple with circles and sidepasses. The other saddlebred was going to be a saddle seat horse, but had to be trained to wear the show bridle which had two bits and two sets of reins. This young mare had a fussy mouth and Jayne was still trying to find the right combination of bits to use on her that would be comfortable for the horse to carry, but to which the horse would be responsive to. She just hadn't figured it out yet and was trying a different mouth piece for the curb bit.

The Morgans were her favorite though. They were smart and enjoyed work and would often try to anticipate what she was going to ask them to do. Mentally, she had to try to think ahead of them so she usually had to be more focused when riding them. She had to keep their training sessions varied so that they wouldn't try to think ahead and they would have to pay more attention to her.

Beth's new Morgan horse, Dallas, was the biggest challenge right now. He liked to throw in a little buck or two when you asked him for a canter and he would wear the bridle well until you made a mistake…. then the nose would go up and he would fight the bridle for several strides until you could get him to relax his jaw and settle with the bridle again. When he flexed his neck, and tucked his nose where it was supposed to be, he was a vision of Morgan horse perfection.

Today however, Dallas was anything but perfect. Jayne just couldn't keep her concentration. She had been focused enough on the other horses to hold everything together, but she just couldn't get Dallas to work with a relaxed jaw at the trot. She decided to pick her battles. She would not canter him today …. if that nose wasn't going to stay tucked for a trot, then it was certainly not going to happen for the canter. Jayne didn't feel like trying to deal with a buck or two either. Maybe she was just tired. He was the 15th horse that day and she was just feeling old today…. old woman. Old …. Tired …. woman. She wasn't getting any younger. The stress of the investigation and her lack of sleep was getting to her.

She had to end on a good note before getting off Dallas though. She made him back slowly down half of the arena and then asked him for a forehand turn. She patted him on the shoulder, gathered her reins and then asked him to back down the arena again, asking for five steps at a time, then ten steps forward. Then five more steps back, then ten more steps forward. The backing was making him tuck his nose and when she asked him to move forward, he maintained the tucked nose without throwing it in the air again. She stopped after a couple of repetitions. He did it, she needed to get off now… before he had a chance to do it wrong and she would have to start over again.

She led Dallas out of the arena. His dark bay coat was almost black with sweat. She rubbed the white lightning bolt marking on his forehead and raised a white, sweaty lather. "Yuck, Dallas. I didn't think we worked that hard." She wiped her hand on his black mane.

Bunny stepped up and took Dallas. She handed Jayne her cell phone. "You just missed a call."

Jayne looked down at her screen, it was Detective Herrero. She went into the office and sat down on the sofa under the ceiling fan. She sank into the soft leather. Was this going to be good news or bad news? Maybe it would be no news. She dialed the phone.

Moments later she put the phone down. No news. Well maybe it was bad news, but it was news that Jayne had expected. None of horses that went through the Ag station, were Gus. Jayne already knew they wouldn't be him, she was firmly convinced that Gus did NOT leave in a horse trailer. No news. No leads. No Gus.

~ ~ ~

The week passed by somehow. Somehow.

Jayne spent most of it in a fog. She was surprised when Friday came and passed. As stressful as the week had been and as busy as her head was, she had expected the week to drag on by but it had not.

Saturday morning the girls rolled in. They had all called during the week and had kept in touch with Beth who had been calling them every time she heard from her aunt.

Beth had written the assignments on the white board outside of the office door in the barn and the whole day was just very well-orchestrated. The girls checked their duties for the day.

Melissa and little Monica were assigned as the prepare grooms for the day. Whoever had that job would have to pull out the next horse, brush the horse and put the necessary equipment on for whatever Jayne had scheduled for that day. Some horses would be ridden by Jayne, some horses would be worked in a ground harness called a surcingle, some horses would be harnessed and Jayne would exercise them from a cart and the lesson horses would be used for teaching students. They started their routine. Monica was too tiny and short to do the saddling and bridling, but Melissa put her in charge of picking out hooves …since little Monica was closer to the ground. Monica was happy with that arrangement as long as she was able to help brush too.

Sarah was assigned as the takeaway groom for the day, when Mrs. Jayne was done working a horse, the takeaway groom would remove the saddle, bridle, surcingle or harness, then they would cool out the horse. In this warm Florida weather, the horses would be rinsed and the excess water scraped off with a special tool and then the horses were put up in their stalls where they each had a fan blowing cool air down at them.

Susan was assigned to cleaning the tack…. wiping down the saddles and girths, soaping and conditioning the leather bridles, wiping the bits off, putting the sweaty saddle pads in the laundry basket to be washed by Bunny during the week, and putting the equipment away.

In between tasks, the girls would pick stalls and dump their wheelbarrows behind the barn at the manure pile. The manure pile would eventually be worked by Jayne's husband Matt. He was not a horse person, but he loved playing with the big tractor on the farm. He would use the tractor to turn over the manure pile so that over time it would break down into fertile dirt, then he would spread it out on the pastures in the summer

66

months where the rains would soak nutrients into the ground but it was too dry right now to do that and the manure pile was growing bigger and higher.

Today, Beth had assigned herself the job of bucket scrubber. She was sitting in a white plastic chair by the barn on the concrete pad of the wash rack where the horses were bathed. She was armed with a scrub brush and a bottle of generic mouthwash and was surrounded by dozens of black plastic buckets. She had turned the hose off and paused her scrubbing. She heard a horse whinny off in the distance, maybe from the preserve, and it reminded her of her Gussie.

She brushed a teardrop away on the shoulder of her tee shirt and then picked up the mouthwash and poured one 'glug' into each of the next two buckets she would scrub. The mouthwash helped to kill the microbes and algae that tried growing in the buckets and was much easier to rinse out of the buckets than soap was. If any residue was left behind after rinsing, the horses detested a "soapy" taste but didn't seem to mind the minty fresh smell and taste of the mouthwash. Beth always liked this job, but now that the weather was getting hotter, she could feel the sun beating down on her and her feet began roasting in her black rubber muck boots.

She slid her feet out of the boots and pulled her socks off. Rolling her riding breeches up her legs, she ran the hose on her skin. The cool water felt good and she let her mind wander. Maybe she would ask Aunt Jayne if they could ride on the trail past the cattle gate and she could swim Gus in the lake …. except … she remembered there was no Gus. Her heart felt heavy in her chest. She dropped the hose and put her face down into her hands and wept.

~ ~ ~

The Pitchfork Princesses were all gathered in the barn office with the door closed. The little air conditioner in the window had been turned on and the ceiling fan was helping to move the cool air around. They were all chattering as they pulled out their lunch bags and settled down to eat.

Sarah opened her bag and pulled out a little orange, then a banana, a can of soda, finally a plastic tub full of lettuce and baby carrots and a packet of vinaigrette salad dressing. "Hey? What the ……. what is this? Where is my FOOD?"

Monica had taken a big bite of her PBJ sandwich and had a line of grape jelly across her lips. "Mfyou haff fwood." She mumbled as she was chewing.

"This isn't FOOD food…. I want my chicken parmigiana, not a salad. Why did mom pack this? We were supposed to have restaurant food leftover from dinner." She looked at her sister Susan who was by the microwave watching the plate inside turn. "She didn't pack a salad for you, you wouldn't be microwaving a salad." She jumped up and went to her sister's side and tried elbowing her out of the way. "YOU HAVE CHICKEN PARM!"

Susan elbowed Sarah right back and smiled sweetly at her twin. "I told mom I would pack lunch today, and since last week you wanted to be a vegan I thought I would give you vegan food." Sarah just looked at her, slack-jawed momentarily. She then lit up the room with a stream of profanities.

Monica gasped and clapped her hands over her ears. "I am not supposed to listen to those words."

"SARAH!" Melissa hissed. "You need to stop!" She also covered Monica's ears.

Sarah marched back to where everyone was sitting and started looking and picking through everyone's lunch bags. "I just want a ham sandwich…. or, or, some mac and cheese,… or ….. something!"

The microwave dinged and Susan opened the door and the cheesy-chickeny aroma wafted through the office. She took out the bowl and then placed another bowl in the microwave.

Sarah had gone to the refrigerator and stood with the door open. "Is this leftover pepperoni pizza from last week? Do you suppose it is still good?"

Susan walked over and nudged her sister. "Here, this is for you." She offered her the chicken. "I brought spaghetti for me, I just wanted to trick you and see you have a meltdown."

"I will have my revenge." Sarah pointed her fork at her sister and snatched the steaming container from her. She marched back to the group.

The girls were laughing when Jayne walked into the office. "What is so funny?" She listened as Monica giggled and hiccupped as she told Mrs. Jayne about Susan's trick. Susan pulled her spaghetti out of the microwave and joined them. Sarah just sat hunched over and bit into her chicken, she started to mumble something but glanced at little Monica and changed her mind.

Jayne went over to the fridge and pulled out a slice of pizza and started eating it. "Mrs. Jayne, eww! Evelyn exclaimed. "You are going to get sick on old pizza."

Jayne looked at the pizza, "This is left over from the pizza Matt and I ordered last night. No worries." She looked around the room then walked over to the bathroom door and knocked. "Beth?"

"She isn't in there," said Evelyn, "she is sitting in Gus's empty stall."

"I'll get her for you Mrs. Jayne" Monica hopped up and wiped her purple grape jelly lips on a napkin.

"No... no. Just leave her for a little bit. She wants to be alone right now." Jayne grabbed a drink out of the refrigerator. "If she doesn't join us in a little bit then I will go see her." She heard a rumble coming up the driveway and peeked out the office window.

"Well I thought I would get a chance to run a quick classroom, but it looks like the hay delivery is here." She unlocked her desk drawer and removed her checkbook and then went and rummaged through her filing cabinet and pulled out a little booklet which she handed to Evelyn. "Evelyn, can you please review horse colors and markings with the girls? I want everyone to start studying for the Youth contest which will be next April in Gainesville. The winner gets a scholarship to compete in Oklahoma at the National show so I thought we should start studying now." She left the office and shut the door behind her.

"Poor Mrs. Jayne," Melissa remarked. "She isn't even getting a chance to sit down to eat in the cool office."

"She has been sitting down all morning." Susan growled.

70

"Sitting in saddles and working horses all morning is not sitting. It is work." Evelyn pointed out. "She works hard and hardly ever takes breaks unless she is teaching us or talking on the phone."

Susan grumbled something that nobody understood or tried to understand.

"Horse Colors." Evelyn interjected. "The first one is 'bay'…. a bay horse has a brown body and black points."

"What are points? Are they ears?" Monica asked.

"No, you impatient girl, let me finish."

"Melissa," little Monica clamped her hands over her ears. "She called me a patient. Is that a bad word?"

"No, take your hands off your ears and listen, we are learning."

"As I was saying ….. bays have black points," she read from the booklet. "The points are the mane and tail and the lower legs. Bay horses will have black legs up to and often including their knees. If they have white leg markings, the black will extend above their white markings. The brown base color can range from a light sandy brown to a gold-brown, to a red brown, to almost black-brown" She paused for the information to sink in. "which horses in our barn are bay?"

Names were shouted out.

"Sophie!"

"Tina and Marley!"

"Dante!"

"Dallas!"

More and more names were called out. As most of the horses at Wildwood were Morgan horses, bays were the most common color in the stable.

"The next color is chestnut," Evelyn continued. "Chestnuts have a basic body color of red or brown and do not have black points and do not have black manes or tails. A chestnut may have a mane and tail of the same color as the body, or a slightly darker shade of brown than the body, or may have a mane and tail several shades lighter than the body, including yellow or almost white. These horses with lighter manes and tails are called 'flaxen' chestnuts." Another pause for the information to soak in, and also to think about Gus. "Which horses in our barn are not flaxen chestnuts, but are regular chestnuts?"

"Copper!"

"Jahil!"

"Red!"

"Kammy!"

"Kammy is not a chestnut!"

"Is too."

"Is not."

"Stop girls. Let's think." Melissa pushed her glasses up her nose. She no longer had the haystring, her parents had bought her a cord for her glasses. "I don't think she has any black on her but she is super dark." They all thought for a minute.

Evelyn interrupted the thinkers. "Let's keep going and we will ask Mrs. Jayne later."

They went on to cover, blacks, grays, roans, pintos and paints, the dilute colors of buckskin, palomino, grulla, perlino, cremello, they touched on appaloosas and then went on to markings ..... stripes, blaze, star, snip, socks, coronets, and ermine marks.

Jayne entered the room and threw her checkbook into the desk drawer and locked it. She flopped down in her desk chair and leaned back, little bits of leafy alfalfa hay were plastered to her sweaty face and neck. "Hot," was all she uttered.

Little Monica picked up the booklet that Evelyn had put down and she stood by Jayne's chair and started fanning her.

Jayne smiled. "That is so sweet but you don't have to do that."

Evelyn went into the refrigerator and pulled out a refrigerated wet baby wipe and walked it over to Jayne. "You have alfalfa stuck to you."

Jayne opened her eyes. "Oh, thank you. I thought I might; it was starting to itch, but I didn't think I could get my arms to work well enough to scratch." She laughed as she sat up. She took the baby wipe and wiped her face and neck.

"Let's clean up in here. All garbage in the outside garbage, I don't want food wrappers or half-eaten sandwiches in the bathroom garbage, ok? Someone threw a half-eaten peanut butter and jelly sandwich in the bathroom garbage last weekend and I ended up with a bathroom full of ants this week."

Everyone looked at Monica, who put her hand over her mouth. Her eyes got really big.

"You are not in trouble," Jayne smiled, "but I don't want it to happen again."

"Everyone saddle up, group lesson today. Beth isn't feeling like doing a trail ride today so afterwards I am going to teach everyone to drive."

"Ohhh, Mrs. Jayne," Monica shook her head. "I think I am too tiny to drive your big truck. Sarah and Susan are too small too."

Melissa scooped up the child. "Driving a horse, silly. We are going to sit in the cart," she looked at Jayne, "right?"

"Right. So off you go!"

# Chapter 9

"I am so glad Beth is riding again." Evelyn leaned on her pitchfork in front of the barn and watched Beth trotting down the arena rail on Dallas. His neck was arched and his nose was tucked down, ears pricked forward. He had a big way of going with his knees popping up with every step. Beth was struggling to not fly off the flat, English cutback saddle that was used for the style of riding called saddle seat. The flaps on the saddle didn't have knee rolls like her jumping saddle had so Beth was fighting to keep her legs steady without the extra support from the saddle.

Beth wasn't riding him in the full show bridle with two bits yet, she was in a work bridle with one bit, but Jayne had hooked up two sets of reins. All of the Pitchfork Princesses had learned to ride with two sets of reins before, except little Monica. The main rein was thicker and held by the rider's whole hand. It had laces for extra grip and was used to steer and stop the horse and pick up the horse's head. The thinner, smooth rein went through the rings of a martingale on the horse's neck, and that rein was held between the fingers and was only used to help keep the horse's nose tucked in.

Sarah stopped pushing the wheelbarrow and set it down. She sat on the edge to watch Beth. "That is a nice horse. I wish I could ride him."

"Just then, Beth took a funny bounce in the saddle and caught Dallas hard in the mouth. Dallas's nose went up and he slowed down his trot as he bounced his nose around in the air.

"That is OK, Beth. Just give your hands forward a little bit, and just do a little left, right, left tickle on his mouth. He is grabbing onto the bit and you just want to gently take the bit back from him. Do not be harsh or he will just fight you more.... there you go, the muscles in his jaw and cheeks are relaxing a bit.... Left, right, left, right, gently .... Now a little more leg and now that his nose is back down more leg .... more ... push him up into his bridle .... that is nice." Jayne watched a moment more. "Now you have to breathe! You are holding your breath and that is making you stiff. Lift your ribs, if you sink your ribs and hunch your shoulders then you will grab your reins too strongly for balance. Focus on your tummy ... strong and tall tummy muscles with your shoulders back should help lift you as you post."

Dallas threw his head up again and Beth stopped him. She tipped her helmeted head back and looked up at the clouds forming in the sky. In the distance, she thought she heard that whinny again that sounded like Gus. It was silly of her to think it was him, it was just someone riding a horse on the preserve. It had been four weeks already. Four weeks with no clue, no sightings, nothing. He was gone. She just hoped he was healthy and happy, wherever he was. She hoped there was a little girl loving on him and brushing him and running him through fields of flowers.

She felt a tear trickle down her face.

Jayne walked up and put a hand on her niece's thigh. "Don't get frustrated. He is a tough ride but nothing you cannot handle. Think of how much he has already taught you."

"I am not frustrated." She wiped away her tears. "I was just thinking of Gus. Sometimes I think I can still hear him. Do you hear him still?"

"I do not, but I am as old as dirt, I don't hear faint sounds that well." She paused, "Sometimes when I leave the house in the morning, I expect to hear him gallop up to the gate to come in for breakfast; then I get sad when I realize I don't hear him."

Beth nodded. She looked across the arena towards the paddock Gus used to go into. A new horse was turned out there this morning, a tiny miniature horse that Jayne bought from a friend. Little Monica had been fussing over the pint-sized mare named DeeDee and earlier had been running back and forth along the fence, with the tiny horse chasing her from the other side.

Monica's parents had picked her up early because they were going to the hospital to meet Monica's new baby cousin that had been born earlier that day. As the car left, the miniature horse ran the fenceline along the driveway and Monica was waving out the back window of the car. Beth heard her high-pitched voice talking to DeeDee but she couldn't make out the words.

Beth and Jayne silently watched the scene and their gazes followed the car to the end of the driveway where it passed through the driveway gate, went under the shade of the tree and turned left, then accelerated as it drove down the road.

Jayne turned towards Beth and checked Dallas' girth.

"Aunt, you know I haven't seen that kid on the bicycle since the day Gus disappeared."

"Mmm," her aunt responded as she took Beth's foot out of the stirrup and shortened the stirrup by one hole. Jayne moved to the other side and did the same to Beth's other foot. "I wonder if the bicycle girl could somehow be related to Gus disappearing, or since she seems to ride around the neighborhood at all hours, maybe she witnessed something that would help us. I will call Detective Herrero. I don't remember if we told him about the person on the bike that has been watching the farm, but you are right, I haven't seen the bicycle person here since he disappeared."

Jayne pulled out her phone. "Now, back to Dallas. I am going to record you so you can see. I don't think you are staying in control of your post and that when you lose your post you grab back on your reins to check your balance. This horse had a BIG motor on his hind end and he gives a huge stride behind. He is pitching you up and you are posting too high; when you go high, you are getting unstable with your balance. That is what we need to work on…. you need to post lower and stay in control of your posting." Beth steered Dallas out of the grass center and onto the dirt track on the arena. "I want you to think about keeping LOW on your saddle. When Dallas pushes you up out of the saddle with his hips, I want you to slightly tighten your thigh muscles and tummy muscles and use those muscles to stop from going up high. Stay in control of your posting trot …. but BREATHE as you do it."

~ ~ ~

As Beth was finishing up her ride, the girls were back in the barn finishing up the last of their stalls. Sarah was cleaning Dallas' stall and her sister Susan was in the next stall which belonged to a new horse that had come to Wildwood Stables.

78

The new horse, Cleo, is one that Jayne had owned a few years ago and had just bought her back. Cleo had been turned out in the round pen for a bit of play-time after her training session and then would be rinsed and put back into her stall once it was cleaned.

Melissa was standing just inside the tack room door where a bridle was hanging from a hook. She had wiped the bridle down with the foamy glycerin soap and then wiped it with a towel. She was picking some crusty, dried horse spit, off of the steel bit so that she could shine it.

Susan should be doing this, she thought. Susan loved to clean bridles and other bits of tack .... but NOOOOO, Susan was picking stalls and listening to music through the ear buds that attached to the phone in her pocket. Melissa's name was listed for tack duty today on the white board.

Melissa grumbled, she disliked having to clean tack. Her bottle of leather conditioner was empty. This was her 6th bridle she had done and there just was not enough left for this bridle which was her last one for the day. She went into the tack room and opened the cabinet and began shifting assorted bottles and sprays and medications around to try to locate another bottle of leather conditioner.

Sarah was cleaning a stall but paused to lean on her pitchfork. Everyone was going to her and Susan's house after the barn to spend the night. Her dad was going to bring some food home from the family restaurant for dinner. She hoped he would bring the meatball stuffed calzones and a bunch of cannoli for desert. Her mouth watered just thinking about it. Her sister would probably ask for dainty little cheese raviolis with spinach. Sarah scrunched up her face and called over the wooden stall wall, "Susan." No answer. "Sue …. Susan ….Susie….. Susan Marie…." still no answer. She was probably still listening to music through her phone's ear buds.

Sarah pulled her phone out of her pocket. She needed to finish this last stall but had to settle the food issue for tonight. She started to send a text then paused and broke into a wicked grin. She turned on her camera and leaned down close to a pile of manure and then took a picture.

Sent.

Seconds later she heard a thump as her sister rested her pitchfork in the wheelbarrow and she mentally pictured Susan taking the phone out of her pocket and looking at it….. 3……2……1…..

"What is this? "Then a few seconds later, "SARAH! Why are you sending me a picture of poop!?!?"

Melissa poked her head out of the tack room. "What? Poop?" She scurried out and over to look at Susan's phone. Evelyn was coming back up the hallway with her empty wheelbarrow and set it down outside the stall and went to have a look also.

"I love you Sarah, but you are one disturbed kid." Evelyn exclaimed.

Sarah bent down and looked at the pile of manure. It was a few hours old and the 20 or so balls were dry when she poked them with her finger.

Next door, Susan deleted the photo and put her phone back into her pocket. She was getting ready to put her ear buds back in but stopped when Melissa asked her a question.

"Do you know if Mrs. Jayne has another bottle of leather conditioner? I used the last of that bottle." Sarah heard Melissa ask Susan.

"There should be a bottle in the cabinet. It was there last week."

Melissa opened her mouth to reply, but was interrupted by Sarah's shout from the stall next door... "INCOMING!"

Sarah waited and she heard a little thud next door. She knew her missile had made contact with someone.

"Oh! Oh! That almost landed in my mouth!" Melissa screeched, "Sarah, how could you?"

Sarah laughed, "sorry, it was supposed to hit Susie."

"What? What did I ever do to have you throw poop at me?"

"This is to get you back for making me that salad for lunch."

"That was weeks ago!"

"Yeah, but I told you I would get you back.... You were not expecting this, were you? I surprised you! Ha ha!"

Seconds later a volley of horse poop balls were being flung over the wall at her by all three girls. Sarah ducked and scooped up manure and flung a double handful over the wall. She heard her sister say something about her hair and then another volley of poop came over the wall. She heard a few plop into the water bucket behind her. Damn, Beth would be mad, she had just done buckets on this side this morning. Sarah got her pitchfork and picked up an entire pile of manure.... about 20 balls if she estimated correctly, and flung the feces overhead with a perfect arc over the wooden wall.

From the sound of it, the whole pile plopped on the floor without hitting anyone. Maybe she overestimated. "Do you give up yet?" Sarah shouted through the wall.

She was met with silence. Was this a trap? Were they waiting for her to show herself to pummel her all at once? She looked all around the stall divider wall but couldn't find any gaps in the boards to peek through. She pulled out her phone and turned her camera on and turned her sound off. She blindly stuck her arm through the bars on the front of the stall and aimed the camera into the next stall; she snapped a couple of quick pictures and pulled the phone out to check it. There was nobody in the stall.

"Hey, girls? Susan?…. Where did everybody go?"

She stepped into the hallway and carefully made her way towards the back of the barn. "In the round pen!" she heard Evelyn shout.

Sarah crinkled up her forehead. Why did they run out to the round pen? Were they going to bring Cleo in? Her stall right now looked like a manure war zone, because…well, it WAS a manure war zone.

Right as she stepped past the last stall, she realized her mistake. Susan and Melissa had been hiding in an empty stall and they shot out and grabbed her from behind, one at each arm. Evelyn rushed in and then grabbed Sarah by the knees and picked her up. Sarah was off the ground.

She kicked and screamed as they carried her behind the barn. Were they going to put her in the round pen? Why would they do that? "Where are you taking me?" she bellowed as she kicked so hard one of her unzipped paddock boots flew off.

The girls just laughed and as they passed the round pen, Sarah realized her destination and her eyes widened. "No! You can't!"

"Oh yes we can!" Evelyn laughed. They stopped and began swinging Sarah. Evelyn counted as they swung, "1…. 2… 3!"

# Chapter 10

Jayne and Beth walked into the barn. Dallas was dripping sweat and the reins had rubbed the sweat into a white lather on his neck. "I will help you untack him, so you can get him cooled off and rinsed." Jayne offered. She looked around. "I wonder where everyone is."

It was at that moment that three girls came racing around the corner and into the hallway. "Hey! No running in the barn!" Jayne shouted as they screeched to a stop with Melissa almost running right into her. Then she saw it. She saw why they were running. If she had been chased by that thing, she would be running too.

It was Sarah. Or some crazed…. thing… that somewhat resembled Sarah.

Sarah skidded to a stop with eyes blazing and teeth grinding in between the profanities she was muttering. Good heavens, where did that girl learn those words? Jayne glanced around for little Monica and then remembered she had left early. She turned back to look at Sarah who had stopped her profane utterings and was loudly breathing through her nose as her lips were now firmly clenched in a straight line and her eyes glittered in anger. She was only wearing one boot and from head down to her stockinged toe she was dirty, but judging by the smell, that wasn't just dirt. Sarah was covered with manure. It was in her hair, it was all over her clothes. There were smudges on her face and arms. "They …." she panted, "threw…. me…. In …. the… manure pile."

Jayne and Beth just stared. Everyone looked at each other, then Beth broke out laughing. One by one, they all started laughing, even Sarah.

Jayne somewhat composed herself, walked up to Sarah and started brushing the crumbly manure off the girl's head. "Oh dear...... I think you need to go into the wash rack and get hosed off. You cannot spend the rest of the day walking around like that, and I seriously doubt your mom would let you into her new SUV wearing horse poop."

"I have a change of clothes you can use. They will be big on you though," Beth offered.

"After you are hosed off, I want you to march into the house and take a shower. Use one of the dark blue towels in the closet. If you leave your dirty clothes in the bathtub, I will wash them for you and give them back tomorrow." Jayne instructed.

Beth took Dallas to the wash rack and the girls took Sarah to the wash rack and they were hosed down next to each other. A few minutes later, while Sarah was showering, Jayne heard about the events leading up to when Sarah was tossed into and then rolled down Poop Mountain.

"Well, Dallas and Cleo cannot go back into dirty stalls, so let's get busy girls." Jayne turned around and began to walk to the feed shed.

"But Mrs. Jayne," whined Melissa, "Sarah is showering and she started it! She should be helping!"

Jayne turned and looked at the group. "If we wait for Sarah to get out of the shower to put the horses up, we will run very late."

Susan's mouth dropped open and then she uttered, "But….but…"

"Butts are for sitting on." Jayne put her hand up to stop their protests. "I will put Sarah on tack cleaning duty for the next three weekends. What do you think about that?

Everyone except Susan thought that was a good idea. Susan didn't think it was harsh enough, but then again Susan liked cleaning tack.

After the girls rode and the horses were fed dinner, they were gathering up their things into their backpacks and bags to go to the DelRizzo house overnight. Jayne put her arm around Beth. "Today is the first day I have seen you laugh in a month."

Beth looked down. "I have decided that I am probably not going to get him back. We are no closer to finding him than the day he left." She looked up at her aunt. "I am just going to imagine that he is happy and loved by a little girl and that he thinks of me whenever someone gives him a peppermint or shares a root beer with him." She paused, "I wonder if he flaps his mouth for whoever is giving him treats now," Beth whispered.

Jayne wrapped her arms around her niece and whispered, "don't give up yet. I just have a feeling he is right under our nose and we are just not looking in the right place. We will find him. Never give up."

~ ~ ~

"You live here?" Beth looked around in awe. "This is practically a mansion!"

Mrs. DelRizzo went straight for the kitchen as they entered the house and Susan and Sarah led the girls across the marble tiled foyer that opened up to the second floor and featured a suspended chandelier. They began ascending the sweeping staircase and from the landing they looked down to where they had all left their barn shoes in the foyer next to the door.

"I'll bet our boots smell really bad. I think I can smell them from here." Melissa crinkled her nose.

"Who would have thought the Poop Princess would live in a palace." Evelyn grinned and Sarah glared at her.

Susan laughed. "it isn't a palace, it is just home. Now let's get our bathing suits on and swim before dad brings us dinner."

Later that evening they were all gathered on the second floor in the entertainment room. Beth and Evelyn were hitting billiards balls around on the pool table, while Susan, Sarah and Melissa were eating popcorn in front of the big TV. The three of them jumped back in their seat cushions when the slasher with the chainsaw in the scary movie jumped down out of the rafters of an old barn to chase his victim.

Evelyn aimed her cue stick and made her shot. As soon as she did, she groaned and dropped her forehead to the table. She didn't want to look as she heard the black 8 ball slowly roll and drop into the side pocket.

"I win!" Beth thrust her pool cue in the air.

"Shhhhhhh!" came the three voices from the sofa. The TV was playing creepy, suspenseful music. Something was about to happen.

"Is this when the chainsaw dude raises it up above his head and lightning strikes him dead?" Evelyn asked.

"Aww, Evelyn," Melissa whined, "why did you have to spoil it?"

Evelyn just shrugged.

"That was pretty mean to do," Beth laughed. She then high-fived Evelyn,

The movie ended and the girls all padded barefoot downstairs to the kitchen. All barefoot except for Susan who had fuzzy, pink slippers on. There had not been any cannoli for desert, so Susan pulled out a tub of ice cream from the huge black refrigerator. They sat down on barstools around the pass-thru area with the black marble counter. The floor and walls were in white and gray and the recessed lighting cast an eerie glow on the girls as their spoons clinked in the glass bowls as they scraped up the last bits of ice cream.

"We have gone over it again and again, Beth. I think Mrs. Jayne is right. Gus couldn't have been taken too far." Evelyn said.

"I wish we could have found the hammer;" Sarah sighed, "then we could have gotten fingerprints."

"Not if the thief wore gloves." Melissa pointed out.

Sarah raised her eyebrows. "I never thought about that."

"Good, then maybe you will forget about the hammer finally," her sister exclaimed and everyone else nodded agreement.

"Maybe tomorrow we can ride the neighborhood," Melissa suggested, "we should ask your aunt."

Beth swiped her finger around the bowl to get the last bit of melted ice cream and she licked her finger. "You know, sometimes I think I hear him off in the distance."

"You mean like his ghost or something?" Sarah asked.

Beth looked at her for a long moment with wide eyes that slowly clouded over with sadness. She slowly stood up, and without saying a word she walked off, leaving the girls and leaving her bowl and spoon on the counter.

"Now you did it." Melissa accused Sarah.

"What did I do? Why is she sad?"

"You were talking about Gus being a ghost, you dummy." Her sister smacked her in the back of the head.

"Ow! What? I thought it was funny?"

"Sarah…" Evelyn shook her head, "for it to be Gussie's ghost, that would mean Gussie was dead. Did you stop to think how Beth would feel about that?"

"Oh. Yeah…..that was stupid of me. I think I was just caught up thinking spooky things because of the movie," she paused, "I will apologize to her."

They all stood up to put their dishes in the washer including Beth's which Evelyn stacked into her bowl to carry. "Don't," said Evelyn, "Beth likes to be alone and if you bring it up she will get mad." She thought for a moment, "haven't you

90

noticed how Mrs. Jayne handles Beth? When Beth gets emotional, Mrs. Jayne just lets her sort it out on her own, and then she goes to her when Beth is calmer. Mrs. Jayne has always done that…. Maybe you should write Beth a note and leave it for her to read later."

Sarah nodded, "I like that idea. I will write a note and draw a picture of Gus."

"NO!" all the girls hissed at her.

"…. or maybe I will draw a picture of a flower….yes, a flower."

~ ~ ~

The next morning, Monica was still having fun with her new baby cousin and was not at the barn so the older girls were rushing to get through their chores. They had asked Mrs. Jayne to skip the lesson so they could spend more time riding the roadsides of the neighborhood instead.

They all saddled up and donned helmets and struck out. They were going to try to eyeball every farm in the neighborhood. The little scouting team wandered up and down every street. Most of the little farmettes had their gates closed, but a couple of the bigger farms were open on Sundays so the girls went up onto those farms and said they were just dropping in for a visit; they were really there to look down barn hallways to see if they could see Gus sticking his head out of a stall. They looked into paddocks and fields and checked out riders, but nobody was riding anything that even resembled Gus.

They were riding up the last road in the neighborhood, Aristides Lane. There was a big and fancy stable at the end with a couple of barns and a huge covered arena. It was the biggest farm in the neighborhood with over 60 stalls in the main barn and a smaller 6 stall barn in the back. It was much bigger than Wildwood which only had 28 stalls.

Aristides Lane was the longest roadway in the neighborhood. As they approached the last little bit of the road, they neared a park area on the right side where there was the Eastern entrance to the Wildwood preserve. The park was a large trailhead and had a paved parking area for trucks and horse trailers, there was a small playground area and bathrooms, and a water spigot for people who wanted to fill water buckets for their horses to have a drink. People from all over the county and beyond would trailer horses over to the trailhead to use the public trails.

The park was just a little bit past the halfway point of this section of road and right before a blind curve. The girls were almost at the park when Melissa saw a glint ahead. She glanced over to see if Beth had spotted it, but Beth was turned around sideways looking at horses and cows in a pasture behind a rickety wooden barn.

"Is that a bicycle up ahead?"

Beth looked to where Melissa was pointing. Ahead of her she could see a white bicycle being leisurely pedaled ahead of them. The cyclist was riding away from them and she had long blonde hair that had been dyed purple at the bottom. She was wearing a white helmet.

"White bike, white helmet." Beth thought out loud. "I am going after her; stay here." She pointed to the park coming up.

"I want to chase her too!" Sarah complained.

"Wait here, don't move." Beth pushed Copper off to the grassy shoulder of the road and urged him into a trot and then a canter. Why did she have to be riding Copper of all horses? He had a slow and dinky canter, does he even gallop? she wondered, then decided to find out. She gave him his head.

Nope. She gave him a bigger kick. This is where Gus would have dug his hind end into the ground and put it into high gear. He could flatten out his short little body and skim the ground so quickly. Copper, despite being much taller than Gus, just took bitty little steps. This was why Aunt Jayne used him for teaching riders how to canter. He had short, choppy strides that were actually smooth to ride to, but you don't get the feeling of going anywhere.

Even then, she was still making up ground on the bicyclist ahead who was lazily pedaling. Beth was catching up…. a little at a time... if Copper would only go faster...

The girl on the bike must have heard Copper's hoofbeats when Beth rode him across a gravel driveway. Without the grass and dirt to muffle the sound, the girl sensed them. She turned her head and at first seemed to slow down as if she was going to stop and talk to them, but then Beth saw her eyes get big and the girl seemed to pedal as if her life depended on it. She started pulling away a little at a time.

Back in the distance behind her she heard Sarah shouting. "Go get her!"

The girl continued to draw away and rounded the corner. Beth was on the wide side of the curve and didn't want to take Copper onto the pavement and she was about 20 seconds behind. She rounded the corner and then started drawing

Copper's reins up and halted. The girl on the bicycle was nowhere to be seen.

Beth stood in her stirrups and frantically glanced all around. She looked up the road and at the little farmhouses that dotted the roadway. There were no bicyclists to be seen, just a series of farmettes and a forested area thick with oak scrub over to her left. There was no way anyone would bicycle through that.

Beth stayed there; she waited. Was someone going to peek out of a house? Would there be a flash of movement in the distance? She waited. She circled Copper but then stopped and looked around some more. Whoever that girl was, Beth knew that the girl was watching from wherever she was hiding. Beth could feel it. She waited, and waited. A few seconds later, Beth made a clucking sound with her mouth to urge Copper to walk, and she slowly walked back to the girls who were impatiently waiting in the park area for her.

~ ~ ~

After the girl on the copper-colored horse disappeared back around the bend, the blonde girl climbed her way down out of a tree. A branch caught her on the way down and she heard a small rip and felt the rough bark abrade her as she dropped the last few feet into the grass. She put her hand over her heart which felt like it was going to explode out of her chest. She quickly reached back into the scrub of bushes and pulled her bike out. A few vines clung and didn't give up the bicycle easily and she pulled at them and ripped them with her hands. She tried to look at the scrape on her elbow. She could feel that her shirt had ripped at the elbow and that her elbow was scraped, but couldn't see it. Her neck was itchy too and her hand came away with blood on it. She thought she had scraped more than just her elbow but didn't have time to think about it.

She pulled some dried leaves out of the purple ends of her long hair and hopped on her bicycle and pedaled as quickly as she could. She had a feeling the girls on horses would still come this way, so she had to hurry and get to her destination before they could see her again. She kept looking back over her shoulder until she knew she was safe.

~ ~ ~

"I was so close, and then she just disappeared." Beth shook her head and gave Copper a pat. He certainly tried his best; he was just the wrong horse for the job. Next time she would have to make sure she was on Sophie. She would fight Sarah for her; Sophie could run. Come to think of it, Jahil could run too. Despite being a Western pleasure horse that was expected to go slow, he could really open up and run. He was low to the ground like Gus was and his short little legs could pump quickly with each stride…yes, Jahil next time.

The girls continued up the lane in silence. Every one of them was keeping a lookout for any kind of movement in any direction. They went around the curve and Beth looked over to the wooded area again. She didn't remember those vines pulled out from the woods and laying in the grass; it seemed as if there had been a disturbance. She halted Copper in pretty much the exact spot she had stopped in before. "This is where I realized I lost her. I looked over there," she pointed to the woods, "but those vines were not sticking out all over the grass before."

Beth stared. "I'll bet she hid in there and watched me until I left." She dismounted off of Copper and leading him, she walked over to the disturbed area. The vines and scrub were thick and thorny. Something caught her eye up above her head in the tree. "I see something."

"Is it a clue?" Melissa peered through her glasses, squinting to try to see what Beth was looking at.

"Is it a hammer? Please tell me it's a hammer!"

"You know Sarah, I think it is a hammer." Beth replied. She pulled Copper closer to the tree and mounted him. Maybe she could reach if she was sitting on his back.

"YESSSSSS! A Hammer!" Shrieked Sarah. "I knew if we looked long enough we would find it!"

"I am just kidding; it's not a hammer."

"Noooooo. Don't tell me that. I want a hammer."

"I'll give you one for Christmas." Beth settled into the saddle on Copper, stood in her stirrups and reached up. Her fingertips brushed the fabric. She couldn't quite reach. She broke off a branch from one of the lower limbs and quickly stripped the leaves off. She knocked the cloth out of the tree and it fluttered down and landed on her thigh. It was about three inches long and an inch wide and had faint, faded lavender polka dots. "I think we have our first clue."

"It should have been a hammer. You can't get fingerprints off of a piece of fabric. Can you?"

Melissa rolled her eyes. "Last time I dropped a hammer, it didn't end up in a tree. Did you really think we would find a hammer in a tree?"

"It could happen," Sarah mumbled and looked away, pretending to adjust her foot in the stirrup.

Susan rode Jahil up to Copper and made a closer inspection of the fabric. "It is a cotton blend of some sort."

"Does that tell us anything?" Evelyn asked.

"I remember when we first started riding last year; Mom took us to the Fox and Hound tack store to shop for riding boots for lessons. I remember seeing some riding shirts that had dots on them like this. There was a pink dot that I wanted," Susan looked at her sister, "and you wanted the one with the green dots."

"I did not; I wanted the blue dots."

"And there was one with purple dots too. They were darker purple than this, but cotton fades. I remember it was this kind of weave, the shop lady said that it was to make you feel cooler when you were riding."

"I don't remember seeing you wearing polka dotted shirts last year." Beth looked at the two.

"Well, we kind of started arguing with each other over which boots we wanted and mom hurried us out of the store. When we went back, they had sold out of everything except the green." Susan said.

"It was a really ugly green," Sarah added, "kind of a brownish green like the camouflage stuff you wear sometimes Beth. You probably would have liked it."

"Umm, probably not. I do camo, not polka dots." Beth pushed the fabric scrap into her pocket. They continued up the road and eventually reached the dead end where the big Foxhill

Farm stood. Their gates were usually open but they were closed today.

"Wow, usually there are a ton of riders out here on Sundays." Melissa reached up under her helmet to scratch her ear. I have neighbors who ride here. They were trying to get me to take lessons here instead of your aunt's place."

"Look, they usually have a big horse trailer parked over on that side of the barn and a big fancy RV too," Beth pointed over to the side, "they must have taken horses to a show. They only take the RV out when they have a big show."

"So, I guess we cannot check them out today, but it looks like they have a bunch of horses turned out," said Susan.

"But no Gus." Beth sighed.

They slowly turned the horses and headed back home.

"The Fox and Hound is closed on Sundays; it would have been nice to go visit them. I will have to see if Aunt Jayne can take me tomorrow."

"You are not going home tonight?" Melissa asked.

"Tomorrow is Memorial Day, there isn't school." Beth pointed out.

The girls all looked at each other and then Sarah asked what they all were thinking. "Do you think your aunt would let us come to the barn tomorrow? My parents don't go into the restaurant until later in the morning, maybe I could get mom to pick everyone up and drive us out there, but someone else's mom or dad would have to pick us up."

Beth shook her head. "I don't know. She only gets one day off each week. She might not want everyone out there when she wants to relax. She was actually thinking of taking me to the beach at Fort DeSoto park."

The girls looked at each other. Mrs. Jayne was looking tired lately. "You are right," Evelyn nodded, "she needs her day off."

# Chapter 11

Uncle Matt and Aunt Jayne slept in late that Monday morning since they both had the day off from work. Beth wandered out to the barn early and helped Bunny and Charlie feed the horses and then turn horses out for the day. They usually worked on Mondays, but Jayne had told them to just feed in the morning and turn out, then in the evening bring horses in and feed dinner, and they could have the rest of the day to themselves to enjoy. With Beth's help, they finished quickly and then the couple walked to the cottage arguing on what they were going to do with their day. Beth had a feeling Charlie would want to go fishing in St. Petersburg and Bunny would want to visit her sister in Tarpon Springs. Beth wondered who would get their way today.

She walked into the house and heard her aunt in the shower. Uncle Matt was absent mindedly eating a crunchy strip of bacon with one hand, as his other hand was holding his tablet. She peeked over his shoulder, he was reading the news.

She kissed him on the cheek and went to the fridge to pull out some cold milk and then pulled her box of cereal out of the cupboard. As she walked to the table, she saw Uncle Matt slip a piece of bacon to his collie; Cora was his dog and that dog worshipped him. Now Beth knew why, it was probably the bacon.

She plopped down next to her uncle and shoveled a spoon of frosted wheat into her mouth and started chewing.

"So, Beth, what are your plans for today?"

"Mmmggh" she chewed a bit more and swallowed quickly. "We are going to check on a clue that I think we found yesterday that might have to do with the horse thief."

"Yes, Jayne told me about the purple fabric. Jayne said she was getting her hair cut this morning first. She wants to shorten it for summer." He paused. Beth spooned another bite into her mouth. "Are you going to go with her to the hairdresser?"

"Yermmff." She gave Uncle Matt a look as she hurriedly, chewed and swallowed. He did not make eye contact and just swiped to the next page on his tablet. Gulp. "Yes. Can I borrow your drone while I am over there? Please?" She waited. Matt looked thoughtful. He was quiet. She kept her eyes on him and slowly raised her spoon to her mouth and slowly started chewing. Matt didn't meet her eyes and continued to look at his screen.

"What do you want it for?"

"Ha! I didn't have cereal on that last spoon, just milk. You were waiting until my mouth was full to ask me a question, you were doing that on purpose! I knew it!"

Matt smiled and then picked up his plate to take it to the kitchen. "You got me. Yes, you can take the drone, just bring it back before you go anywhere else." His cell phone rang and he turned to answer it. Beth picked up her spoon and took another bite and started chewing. "Her uncle handed her the phone. "It is for you."

Beth snatched the phone, and Matt ran across the kitchen towards the back bedroom; Cora ran behind him and followed him a little too closely as he headed into the hallway … and that slowed him down just enough for the spoon Beth threw at him to make contact with his back before clattering to the tile floor.

Cora picked up the spoon in her mouth and with a doggy smile, she trotted after her master wagging her tail as she disappeared after him into the bedroom.

~ ~ ~

Thirty minutes later, Beth and Jayne pulled up in the driveway one block over and four houses from the corner where the girls always turned to access the western entrance to the Wildwood Preserve. The property was about 4 or 5 acres and was a long and skinny property with the house sitting fairly close to the road. The house had a chain link fence in the front yard but the back yard was separated from the front with brown wooden stockade fence on either side of the house. Beth watched as a white chicken squeezed through a broken bottom board on the wooden gate.

This must be the house that is just down from the goat place, the house with the purple-striped curtains on the back, corner bedroom. She remembered the stockade fence that ran all the way down the sides of the property to the wire back fence on the preserve. She also remembered seeing a bunch of chickens in this particular yard. A lot of people around here had chickens, but this was the only place she knew of that had White Leghorns and Buff Orphingtons. Everyone else seemed to have Rhode Island Reds, black Australorps and also the Americaunas which laid the blueish eggs. Everyone seemed to have those but this property had different chicken breeds.

Jayne grabbed her purse out of the truck. "Are you going to come in Beth?"

"No, I think I will sit in the back of the truck and fly Matt's drone around to see what I can see."

"OK honey, but if it gets too hot, please come into the house where the air conditioner is."

Beth was only half listening and answered "OK" but she was focused on bringing out the big gray airship. She closed the truck door with her leg as she turned around with both arms laden with Matt's drone and the remote. Another chicken popped it's head out through the fence boards and then popped back behind the fence. There was a big round metal garbage can set by the house with a gray cat sitting on it. He stared at Beth with his yellow eyes and then turned and jumped down and disappeared through the broken piece of fence. That is when Beth noticed bicycle handlebars sticking up behind the metal can.

She carefully picked her way over the paver stones to where the garbage can sat. She caught the edge of a paver with her toe and almost tripped so she put the drone and remote down in the grass and continued towards the side of the house to get a better look at the bicycle. It was the ugliest bicycle she had ever seen. It had been propped up against the side of the house behind the garbage can and the bike was just metal colored, and that metal was all scratched and scraped up.

Sitting with the bicycle was a beige plastic grocery bag that was almost translucent but not quite. It seemed to have little bits and flakes of white matter in it. Was that paper? Sitting in the grass by the bicycle tire was a hammer.

Beth stifled a laugh. If Sarah was here she would be jumping up and down thinking she had found "THE HAMMER." It is a good thing she and the other girls were not there.

She picked the drone back up and climbed into the bed of the truck. She made sure not to trip over the ball hitch in the middle of the truck bed and she sat down on the toolbox behind the cab. She picked up the remote and the drone propellers began to whir. Beth piloted the drone up, higher and higher until she cleared the trees before she began to steer it. It wobbled a bit but she then straightened it out. She looked at the screen to see what the drone's camera was picking up. She saw the cows across the street. From the height of the drone they almost looked like pinto horses, but the little herd were all black and white milk cows with one that was red and white. She hovered the drone and turned it around, she could see herself sitting in the truck, but then she also saw a horse in the yard behind the house. He was down at the far end of the yard by the fence that separated the yard from the preserve.

She didn't remember this house having a horse in the yard. Never on any of the trail rides did she ever see anything other than chickens. The horse appeared to be eating out of something. Beth steered the drone until she was almost directly over the horse and she dropped the drone down about 30 feet lower. The horse was eating out of a round rubber feed pan and a flake of hay was sitting next to the pan. The horse had a dark mane and tail. Beth remembered Detective Herrero saying that two horses were new to the neighborhood from their door to door inquiries last month. One was a bay and the other was an appaloosa. This must be the bay he referenced.

She raised the drone back up and followed the back fenceline. She passed over the house with the goats and two huge white dogs ran under the drone; she could hear them barking. She flew over the preserve. She could see people riding on the trails, but Beth knew better than to fly low over horses being ridden. She didn't want to spook any horse and have riders or horses injured, but that group out on the trails consisted of a gray horse, two dark bays and a pinto. She didn't need to get closer.

It was a holiday; there were probably a lot of people out riding this morning. Kids were off school and so many people were off work. As she flew back over the neighborhood, her theory was right. There were lots of people out on the roadways in their golf carts, and lots of children on bicycles or playing ball in the street, and many people were out riding their horses. She didn't want to fly too low as it would scare some horses, but she was low enough that if a red horse with a white mane and tail appeared on screen, she would be able to see it well enough. Now she just hoped one would appear.

She had sweat trickling down her back. She had a tee shirt on over her bathing suit and she could feel the shirt starting to stick to her. She could hear the hair dryer inside the house. That meant her aunt would probably be done soon so she quickly steered the drone back and it soon appeared down the road a little ways and Beth stood up. She carefully landed the drone on the open tailgate of the truck. She sat down and was about to hop out the back of the truck when she heard the screen door on the house slam and then the scraping sound of the metal garbage can lid being lifted. She quietly stood back up in the bed of the truck and looked over the cab. A girl with shoulder length blonde hair had her back to her. Beth watched as she threw what looked like a rag into the garbage and then went over to the bike and picked up the plastic grocery bag and tossed it into the garbage too. She replaced the lid and started dragging the metal can across the grass. Beth watched while she dragged the can past the truck and towards the curb.

The girl didn't even notice Beth in the truck. Beth watched the girl. Her blonde hair contrasted with the purple tie-dyed tee shirt she was wearing. "Hey you, stop!" Beth called out to the girl.

The girl looked up and froze when she saw Beth. Her eyes opened wide and she just stood there, apparently holding her breath.

"What are you doing? …. It is Memorial Day; the garbage men are not coming today."

The girl stared at Beth and without blinking she silently nodded her head and then looked down at the metal can. She dragged it back up to its spot next to the house and then she hurriedly opened a gate in the fence, gave Beth a quick glance, and disappeared into the yard.

What a strange person, Beth thought.

~ ~ ~

"My head feels so much lighter!" Jayne exclaimed.

"You will feel so much cooler this summer." Karen said. "But I am not finished drying it yet. Let me look for my round brush, I want to roll your layers a little as I blow dry so I can put a little more body in your hair, you know. ……Oh, let me add a little mousse from that new product line, I think you will like it…."

"Oh Karen, that won't be necessary. My niece and I are headed to a shop and then will be on our way to the beach. Mousse will just get sticky in the heat and I will end up with who knows what stuck to me.... probably a lot of sand and that would itch."

"Of course. But let me at least dry it for more.... poof." She made little poofy motions with her hands and then continued to rummage in her drawer. Jayne pulled her hand out from under the plastic hairdresser's poncho and checked her phone's web browser. She pulled up the Fox and Hound tack store; she hoped they would be open today. Their page on social media did not indicate that they would be closed for the holiday, and their normal hours showed they opened at 10 on Mondays. They would get there shortly after opening if they were lucky.

As Jayne looked at the phone, Karen saw her daughter Caitlyn walk by with a torn shirt. "Oh Cait, can you cut me a rag off of that shirt if you are throwing it away? I want a nice rag to wipe my mirror." Caitlyn picked up scissors from her desk where she did homework. She knew better than to use her mom's hair cutting shears. She snipped a big square off the ruined polka dotted shirt and handed it to her mom, then went out the front door to throw the rest in the garbage.

Karen shoved the rag into the drawer as she finally found the round brush that she wanted. She turned on the hairdryer again and Jayne clicked her phone screen off and tucked her hand back under the Poncho and looked up in the mirror and smiled at Karen as she fluffed.

A few moments later Beth entered and sat down. Her elbow knocked over a display of beige bottles with green tops and she managed to catch them before they rolled off the rickety table. The lady wielding the hairdryer over her aunt's head didn't appear to hear it over the whine of the dryer. Beth set up the bottles and picked up one of the brochures that was on the table in front of the displayed bottles.

Botanical hair products. They must be the ones that make that detangler spray her aunt had. There was a full line of stuff …. shampoo, conditioner, and hair dye, in addition to the detangler. She looked at the list of colors…..there were three shades of red, it looked like about five shades of brown, three shades of blonde and then a blue black and a dark black. They also had fun colors. Turquoise blue, emerald green, hot pink, lipstick red, dark amethyst purple, and an electric blue. Beth wondered what the green and the blue would look like with her dark blonde hair. Maybe she could get her hair colored for fun when school was out for summer.

The hairdryer stopped and the hairdresser whipped the poncho off of Jayne and Jayne looked at herself in the mirror as she stood up. "Karen, I love it. Not too short, but it feels so much cooler already."

Her aunt paid and smiled at Beth. "Well, how did it go; did you see anything?"

"Not really, I saw the bay behind this house, and the appaloosa is over at the place on Aristides before the trailhead."

"Oh, at the Thompson's farm with the red barn?"

"No, across the street with the brown wood barn."

"I don't know them. I thought that place just had miniature horses."

"Well they have a leopard appaloosa horse now too." Beth opened the door for her aunt, "I can't wait to get to the Fox and Hound; I had been feeling hopeless, but with this scrap of fabric, I feel that we are just so close. Like Gus is practically right under our noses."

"I hope you are right."

# Chapter 12

"I remember those shirts; they sold out very quickly... except for the ones with green polka dots." The owner at Fox and Hound said. She looked to the back of the store, "I might even have a couple still over on the clearance rack. Should I show you?"

"No!" Beth and Jayne both replied.

Beth breathed in deeply; there was just something about the way a tack store smelled. The smell of new leather bridles and saddles was just so wonderful. "Do you know which customers bought the purple dotted shirts?"

"It was so long ago dear, and the pink and purple sold out the first weekend after they came in. Those were the two most popular colors. The blues took a few more days. It was a limited run so we didn't get a chance to order more of them in. I would have loved to order another shipment.... except for the greens." She wrinkled her nose.

Beth looked dejected. They started to head out of the shop. They were almost to the door when Beth stopped. She turned and looked at the clerk. "There is a girl, a year or two younger than me with long blonde hair with purple tips, have you seen her in here?"

The shopkeeper's eyes brightened up, "yes! She was in here about 3 or 4 weeks ago. She must like purple; she bought a purple nylon halter and leadrope and I remember she was trying to find a purple bareback pad, but she had to settle for black. I remember her definitely." The shopkeeper nodded.

111

Jayne looked at the shopkeeper, "do you know this customer's name?"

The shopkeeper shook her head. "No I have seen her in here a time or two, but she isn't a regular customer."

Beth looked at her aunt as they walked across the parking lot. "The girl on the white bike with the purple hair that I saw yesterday…. I am thinking she is the one that was watching us, I am certain, and she bought equipment here right after Gus disappeared. The bicycle girl hasn't been seen in front of Gus' paddock since he disappeared, AND when I saw her riding her bike on the road, she raced away from me and hid. She has to be the one who has Gus…. I feel it." Should she dare start to feel hopeful?

Jayne grabbed Beth by the arm, "I feel it too!"

They never made it to the beach. They went back to the barn and pulled out Jayne's notebook. They scribbled down more notes and slowly drove the neighborhood over and over again, several times during the day hoping to see a girl with purple hair on white bike. They flew the drone two more times hoping that someone would be riding a flaxen chestnut on the holiday. Nothing.

Gus had to be in the neighborhood, but who had him? Which of the over 100 properties was he on and where was he being hidden?

The sound of a motorcycle pulling up to the barn made them look up. Jayne looked at the time. "Oh, I promised your dad I would have you home. We have to leave shortly."

They headed out to the barn. Charlie had pulled up to the house he and Bunny occupied at the back of Wildwood Stables. Bunny's car was already parked on the side and Bunny came out of the house to greet Charlie. They walked over to the barn and Charlie headed to the turnouts where the horses were all gathered by the gates wanting in. Bunny went to the feed room and began putting the prepared buckets in stacks in the wheelbarrow. Charlie then headed into the barn leading Dallas.

"So, Charlie, what did you and Bunny end up doing with your almost day off?" Jayne asked.

"Oh, the missus took the car over to Tarpon Springs to visit her sister and they had lunch at one of the Greek restaurants on the sponge docks. I packed up my fishing gear and headed to the Skyway pier on the Harley," he laughed, "I got a lot of strange looks with my fishing pole sticking up off the motorcycle."

"I bet you did. Did you catch anything?" Beth asked.

"I sure did, I reeled in a few grunts that I threw back and then I hooked a snook off the base of the pier, he was a big one and broke my line. Then I reeled in a shark that I threw back because he was too big for me to bring back on the Harley."

Beth mentally tried to picture Charlie with a shark on the motorcycle behind him and laughed.

"It was a relaxing day spent feeding the fish." He smiled as he took off Dallas' halter and shut the stall door.

Beth and Jayne helped Charlie bring in the remaining horses and by the time they finished, Bunny had passed out all the grain and was filling water buckets. Charlie wheeled the big wheelbarrow over to the feed room and stacked up two bales of hay.

"I have to drive Beth home this evening, her parents couldn't pick her up as they had an event to go to. Thanks you two; after you feed dinner hay, leave some small flakes out and I will drop them later this evening during night check."

Jayne and Beth climbed into the truck and headed across town to Beth's house.

~ ~ ~

In the morning between working horses, Jayne stopped for a drink. She checked her phone, it was 8:30. She had 5 more horses to ride but she was slightly ahead of schedule so she dialed up Detective Herrero to fill him in on their weekend events and discoveries.

The Detective did not pick up and his phone went to voice mail. He had taken advantage of the holiday for a quick vacation and wouldn't be back until Thursday. She left him a message telling him to call her when he returned so she could give him updates.

She finished working her horses right before lunch. She had been up in the barn by 5 am and on her first horse at a quarter of 6. All of the horses had worked well so she kept their workouts a little shorter. She went down the aisle and treated everyone to peppermints and then went in the house to shower and make herself a sandwich for lunch. She threw some stuff in the crockpot to heat up for dinner tonight, and then she ran the robotic vacuum cleaner before throwing bed linens in the washing machine.

She sat for a few minutes and then the alarm on her phone buzzed. It was a quarter to three. Her afterschool lessons would be coming out soon so she headed back out to the barn. She would have to give Beth a call later to tell her the Detective was out of town.

# Chapter 13

The girls finished their stalls quickly that Saturday and immediately after their lesson they filed out of the driveway, turned left under the tree at the gate, and headed down the road. Beth made sure she was on Jahil this time and little Monica was riding Copper. Copper was not a Western horse, but he was carrying the little Western saddle on his back and Monica just had to ride him in his English bridle and steer him two handed. She wasn't happy but the girls told her that it was good practice for her and that stopped her from complaining.

The little group walked the grass on the shoulder of the road; Beth wanted to ride back down Aristides Lane and hope to see the white bicycle with the girl with purple tips on her hair. She would run her down this time. As they walked, Beth's phone rang. It was her aunt.

Detective Herrero had finally called back and Jayne had told her about the girl on the bicycle with purple hair. He was going to send officers out door to door again on Monday to see if anyone knew anyone with that description. MONDAY! Beth did not want to wait until Monday to find out who the purple haired girl was.

They chatted as they walked along. They rounded the curve in the road and Beth automatically looked over to the bushes as they passed by. They continued on but no purple haired girl on a bike appeared.

They reached Foxhill farm and the gates were open; the horse trailer and RV were both in their spots. The girls headed up the driveway and passed the arena where a big group lesson was going on. There were three round pens, but they were made of metal pipe fencing, not wood like the one at Wildwood. All three of the round pens had riders in tall boots, breeches and helmets. Each rider was wearing a dark green polo shirt with the barn logo embroidered on the front and they were lunging their horses.

Melissa nodded at one of the girls. "That is my neighbor in the round pen on the left" she told the group. Melissa's neighbor was lunging a massive light gray horse with a darker gray mane and tail. There were faint dapples on the horse's haunches and his lower legs were darkish also. That horse was probably born as a bay and then turned lighter. All gray horses are born dark and then turn lighter as they got older; some grayed faster than others. This was a handsome horse and Beth was certain he was an expensive one too.

Beth knew a few of the girls there and they stopped and chatted. The girls all wished Beth luck in finding her pony. Off in the distance she saw a scraped metal bicycle leaning up against the back barn. There was a girl with shoulder length blonde hair leading a pinto pony into the barn. Beth wasn't sure but from a distance, she looked like the girl from the hairdresser's shop. Beth watched her disappear into the barn. "Who is that in the back barn?" She asked.

"That is Caitlyn. She works here so she can earn money to feed her pony that she just got."

"Was that her pony?"

The girl laughed, "no we haven't seen her pony; she doesn't keep it here. Her mom cuts hair for money and they can't afford to keep a horse at this farm. She keeps it in her backyard."

So that was her; the girl with the bay horse in her yard.

Interesting…. And she rode a bike to the farm to work…. and she worked on Aristides Lane where they saw the bicyclist last week.

This was very interesting.

"Let's go," she abruptly told he girls, "I need time to think." They headed back down the driveway and onto the road. Beth was deep in thought and her head was spinning. Deep in her core, Beth felt that they were close…. very close to finding Gus. This blond girl at the hairdresser's shop was involved somehow, but her pony was a bay. Beth had seen the pony with the drone; this was not making sense. The girls were all quiet as they rode.

Little Monica piped up as they passed by the trail head after rounding the bend. "Beth, when are we going to go out on the trails?"

"Yeah Beth, we have not been on the trails since Gus disappeared. We have been riding the road for weeks," Susan pointed out.

Sarah turned around in her saddle, "We are riding the roads every weekend because we are looking for clues…. like THE HAMMER."

Evelyn looked at Beth and shrugged. Beth checked the time on her phone; they might be able to squeeze in a short ride, but she was not going to take them through the busy trail head. Jayne didn't allow anyone on this side of the trail without adult supervision because of how busy it was and because it was open to the public.

"Let's see how we do on time, maybe we can take a short ride when we are over at the smaller preserve entrance."

This was met with cheers. They moved their horses out of their leisurely walk into a bit of a more ground covering walk. It wasn't long before they were a block away from their stable and Beth drew Jahil to a stop so abruptly that Susan riding on Bodie almost crashed into Jahil's rear. "Why are you stopping? The trail is right around the corner."

"I am thinking," replied Beth, "that girl at the back barn at Foxhill lives here.

"So?" asked Susan.

"So, she rides a bike to Foxhill to work; I was here on Monday and it is metal colored…. like it doesn't have any paint."

"Maybe she is the white bicycle girl and she scraped the paint off of the bike?" Melissa suggested.

Beth snapped her head around, "there was a hammer in the grass next to the bike."

"She has a HAMMER!" Sarah exclaimed, "she is our thief!" She paused, "MAYBE…. she used the nail pulling claws to scrape the paint off her bike….white paint." She nodded.

Evelyn slanted her eyes at Sarah. "Everyone around here has a hammer…. or two even, because everyone around here has to put up, tear down or fix fence a gazillion times each year; and, every kid that lives on these farms around here has a bike."

"A bunch of them have golf carts though, but the ones that don't have golf carts have bikes or scooters." Melissa added.

"But it COULD be her, she has a pony in her back yard." Susan came to her sister's defense.

Beth's mind was working furiously; she was trying to put the pieces of this mystery together. "The girl threw a plastic bag that looked like it had shreds of paper into the trash can, but it could have been paint chips from the bicycle." Beth paused and she ran the memory of that day further through her mind. "Her mother colors hair and has a purple hair dye too."

Susan's eyes got big. "Did the girl you saw with the trash can here have purple hair?"

"No, she didn't, but her hair was blonde and it was shorter."

"Maybe after you saw and chased her last weekend she cut the ends off..." Susan pondered.

"I fell asleep with gum in my mouth and it ended up stuck in my hair and my mom had to cut my hair to get the gum out, see?" Monica pulled her dark ponytail around and showed off a jagged section. The older girls were deep in thought and nobody answered little Monica.

"And then after she cut her purple ends off, she used the claws on the hammer to scrape the paint off her bike!" Sarah exclaimed, "so we wouldn't recognize her!"

Evelyn looked Beth in the eyes. "What if this is it? What if this is where Gus is?"

Beth shook her head. "I have seen the pony; he is a bay. I flew the drone over here on Monday when I waited for Aunt Jayne to get her hair cut. I only saw him from above, but you could definitely tell he was a bay." She paused; she knew the pony living here had a black mane and tail, but something was pulling her, drawing her, compelling her to go look at the horse. Then she wondered out loud, "I wonder if we can see him from behind the house on the preserve?"

Beth stared at the house. Evelyn and Melissa shared a glance and then walked their horses to the lead and urged everyone to follow. Beth held Jahil back as he tried to follow the other horses.

"Beth, are you coming?" asked Melissa.

Beth stood there. "I am afraid. I think this is the closest we have been and all the pieces of the story might be falling into place, but I am afraid to get excited and to get my hopes up and then not find him."

Evelyn rode Magic back and turned so that she was next to Beth and Jahil. Reaching out, she took a hold of Jahil's rein next to the bit and urged Magic on. "Beth, you are coming with us."

They walked to the corner of the road and turned right to head north towards the entrance to the preserve. They all slowed down to walk the horses one at a time over the grid of poles on the ground at the entrance. They were there to prevent people from taking dirtbikes and four-wheelers onto the preserve, but people and horses could just walk over them. They then turned right to head east and follow the fence line at the back of the properties.

They rode on in silence; Beth could hardly breathe. They were coming up to the yard with the wooden stockade fence and then they passed the wooden fence; they pulled up next to the wire fence and saw the long, skinny yard with the white and buff chickens pecking around. There were makeshift jumps set up, constructed out of cinder blocks with boards across the tops, another jump was made of old wooden pallets leaning up against some buckets that were on the ground. There had been a horse here at some point, but the yard appeared to be empty except for the chickens. A faint breeze swept through and a set of windchimes behind the porch could be heard tinkling faintly above the sound of the clucking chickens. The breeze swept across her face. It felt nice and there was a coolness to it. Beth glanced up. There might be a bit of rain tonight.

"Yuck, look at those jumps made from garbage!" Susan exclaimed.

Melissa shook her head, "definitely not safe."

"I would hate to have the horse stop at the jump and for me to fall on that." Sarah scrunched up her face at the thought.

Beth felt Jahil tense up, and turn his head towards the yard. He put his tiny chestnut ears up and stared into the yard, then let out a whinny that shook his whole body.

From up higher in the yard, the whinny was answered.

Beth's heart skipped a beat, then started racing. She recognized that voice. "Gus!" Beth cried out, "Gussie!"

Another whinny answered her and the girls heard the sound of pounding hooves coming back from behind what appeared to be a shed and the chicken coop. A flash or red appeared and a large pony came racing down the property towards the fenceline where the girls were standing. Beth's heart dropped as she saw the streaming black mane and tail. The pony turned along the back fence and came down out of his run to strut into a springy trot with his neck arched and tail flagging. He kept nickering and whickering. Jahil, Copper, Sophie, Kammy, Bodie and Magic watched and nickered greetings back to the pony.

"It is not him." Evelyn turned her head away to hide her tears. She had been so hopeful. She wanted to be hopeful for Beth, and hopeful for Gus.

The girls were quiet. They watched the pony trot back and forth. "He moves just like Gus." Beth lamented.

"He does move like him, doesn't he?" Melissa observed, "he has that big white blaze on his face, he shows the whites of his eyes and he has four white socks. He is pretty flashy......Except for the black mane and tail, he could be Gussie's double."

"What a horrible color," Sarah exclaimed. "He looks…. he looks… like Halloween."

This made the girls chuckle. "I don't think I have ever seen a bay that looked that…. orange, with a mane and tail THAT black…..He does look like Halloween," laughed Melissa, "if Halloween wore a purple halter……yuck."

Beth just stared. The pony had stopped and was pressing his chest up to the fence and arching his long neck out towards them. He shook his head up and down and flapped his lips at Beth.

The girls stared and then all eyes turned towards Beth. All eyes except Monica who tilted her head sideways and looked at the oddly colored pony.

"He is not a bay," little Monica exclaimed. "Remember the book of horse colors that we had to learn? Bays are supposed to have black legs, but I don't know what color he is." Monica started mumbling various colors and counting them off on her little fingers, "not a chestnut, not a bay, not a gray, not a pinto….."

"She is right," whispered Melissa. "He doesn't have black above his white socks. His legs go from white to orange."

Beth slipped off of Jahil and handed the reins to someone; she wasn't sure who was next to her that took the reins, She had her eyes focused on the pony who pricked his ears and watched her approach then resumed flapping his lips at her.

Was this her pony? Had someone stolen him and then disguised his white mane and tail with black hair dye so he wouldn't be recognized? This is the hairdresser's property and she did have hair dye. Could it be?

She hesitated before touching him. She looked at his face, at his eyes. She ran her hands over him and he made little happy whicker sounds. She held her breath as she slid her hand down his neck and lifted his mane. There it was, a little white spot where his crest met the mane. Beth rubbed it; it always was a lucky spot.

The white spot disappeared in a blur as her eyes filled up with tears. She slid her hands around his head and hugged his face. "My Gussie!"

# Chapter 14

Beth wouldn't leave. Gus was here and she was not going to let him leave her eyesight. She tried calling her aunt with her cellphone, but Jayne was not picking up.

Melissa and Monica stayed with Beth; Evelyn, Susan and Sarah wheeled their horses around and rushed to Wildwood Stables at a canter. They were never supposed to canter on the roadside but they didn't think Mrs. Jayne would mind this time. They only slowed down to cross back over the ground poles at the preserve entrance so the horses could pick their way through the grid of poles, then they resumed their canter home.

Back in the barn, Jayne was pulling the water hose down the hallway and was topping off the horses' water buckets. It was so hot and they were drinking huge quantities. So many of the other barns used automatic waterers that filled up as the horses drank, but Jayne had learned the importance of knowing exactly how much the horses were drinking. A horse that didn't drink enough could get colic, and with automatic waterers, she would never really know how much water the horses were drinking.

Colic was a bad stomach ache that could easily be deadly to horses. If Jayne noticed that a horse wasn't drinking enough water out of his buckets, she would add extra salt to their food to try to make them drink more. By the look of things, she had nothing to worry about. Buckets that had been filled to the brim at lunch, were halfway down because the heat was making the horses very, very thirsty.

She heard the clatter of hooves cantering quickly up the driveway. Those girls know better than to run the horses home. She turned the nozzle on the hose off and exited the front of the barn, prepared to scold the girls.... but there were only three of them, and Sarah was all scraped up with a twig and leaves poking out of the air vents on her helmet.

"What happened? Where are the others? Are you all right Sarah?"

Sarah nodded as she tried to catch her breath. Evelyn and Susan were talking over each other and Jayne couldn't make out what they were saying, but they were both somehow talking about Gus, that much she could make out.

"Settle down......what about Gus?"

Sarah wheezed out triumphantly, "we found him! .... and Sophie bucked me off into a bush on the way back, I need a bandage." She pointed to a scrape on her wrist and went to the first aid kit on the wall and pulled out a bandage.

Jayne clapped her hand over her mouth. "Where? Is he OK? Where is Beth, where are the other girls?"

"At the haircutting lady's house," Evelyn said, "we tried calling you."

Jayne hurriedly patted down her pockets and didn't have her phone.... "I left it in the office on the desk. I need to call Detective Herrero." She started for the office, took two steps and then wheeled around. "Unsaddle and put the horses in the paddock. They will eat their grain when we get back." She

128

turned back around and rushed into the office to call the Detective.

The girls hurriedly unsaddled and unbridled the three horses and put them out in the paddock. Their food was already in their stalls, but they were too hot to eat. Eating grain while hot could also cause a colic so they would cool down in the paddock before they would be allowed to eat their grain.

The horses were happy enough to nibble on the dried grass as they slowly cooled off. The girls returned to the barn and Jayne was on the phone, this time to her husband. "......and the girls say they found him, Detective Herrero will meet us there…. finding paperwork…. Beth is with him…. love you, have to go."

Jayne exploded out of the office with a yellow paper in a clear plastic sleeve, and several flyers with Gus's photo on it.

"Into the truck!" she commanded.

They all piled in and strapped on their seatbelts. Jayne fumbled around patting her pockets, then unbuckled her seat belt, jumped out of the truck and ran back into the barn. She quickly appeared with the truck keys in one hand and the scrap of fabric in her other hand, she had remembered to grab the fabric at the last minute when she picked the keys up off her desk. She jumped back in her driver's seat and quickly backed the truck, turned and headed down the driveway; the truck tires slipped in the gravel at the end of the driveway and then squealed as they hit the pavement by the gate and she turned left.

The girls had Jayne drive down and park by the preserve entrance. They hopped over the poles on the ground and ran down the trail with their legs trying to push their way across the soft sugar sand on the trail. Jayne could see the other girls up ahead. Beth was feeding hand-picked grass to the ugliest colored horse she had ever seen. That was Gus?

They reached Beth. 'Aunt, it's Gus! Look," she showed her the lucky white spot on his neck.

Jayne's mouth dropped open as she looked the horse up and down.

"Mrs. Jayne, what color is a bay horse that doesn't have black legs?" Asked little Monica as she stifled a yawn. Oh dear, it was getting late and was almost dark.

"Honey, we will figure it out later." Jayne didn't want to explain it right now.

She had known... she had just known that Gus was still nearby; she had sensed it to her very core, but she didn't realize exactly how close he had been...this whole time! For the first time since he had disappeared, Jayne felt …. relief. Now she could feel happy tears start to roll down her cheek. She hugged Beth and then the other girls not on horses joined in the group hug. Everyone was sniffling.

"I am going to drive up to the front of the house, Detective Herrero is on duty this weekend and he said he would meet me there. You girls all stay here." Jayne started to leave, then turned back to Gus and pulled a peppermint out of her pocket. Gus flapped his lips at her and she popped the red and white candy into his mouth.

~ ~ ~

Jayne saw that Detective Herrero was already there and had parked his gray, unmarked police cruiser in the driveway. Jayne parked across the street and Herrero turned around towards her as he heard her truck door close.

Jayne rushed up and grabbed him by the sleeve. "I saw him; it is him!" Her other fist held the flyer and the yellow paper in the clear plastic sleeve.

Karen answered the door and smiled at Jayne but gave a worried look at Detective Herrero. "Is everything OK Jayne? You are as white as a sheet!"

"Mrs. Green, may we come in? I have a few questions," the Detective asked.

Mrs. Green nervously showed them in the door, and peeked down the road before closing the door behind them.

"Is your daughter home?" asked the Detective.

"No, she had to work today at Foxhill and tonight is her night to help feed dinner to the horses. She should be home soon; I just turned the oven on." From their spot in the living room, Jayne heard the ticking of a kitchen timer coming from further back in the house.

"Mrs. Green, I need to ask you some questions about your daughter and the horse you have in your yard."

Mrs. Green looked puzzled. "But you asked us about him weeks ago, I told you that someone gave him to my daughter."

"Do you know the name of this person? Have you met or spoken to this person? Did any paperwork change hands?"

Mrs. Green was quiet for a long moment with a puzzled look on her face. "No. I don't think so."

Detective Herrero looked at Jayne, then turned his attention to Karen again. "Does your daughter have a white bicycle, white helmet and purple ends to her hair?"

"She does have a white helmet. Her bicycle was white but she wanted to paint it and she has been stripping it. We were going to go to the hardware store after dinner to pick out paint so she could paint it tomorrow ...... I did dye her tips purple a few weeks ago, but she asked me to cut it off recently. She said the school didn't want her hair purple and that she had lost the principal's note."

Jayne and the Detective exchanged a look and Jayne slipped him the piece of fabric that she pulled from her pocket. "I told you about this on the phone."

Detective Herrero looked at the scrap of fabric. "Do you recognize this." He showed Mrs. Green the strip of white fabric with the faded purple polka dots.

"How did you get that?" she looked puzzled.

Jayne heard her phone ring. She looked at the screen, it was Beth. She declined the call and quickly typed a "Not yet" message to her. She guessed that Beth was wanting to know when she could come around and get Gus.

As she sent the text, the Detective explained to Mrs. Green about the girl on the bicycle watching the riders, then racing away from Beth as she tried to stop her to question her. He explained how the scrap was found when the girl hid from Beth.

"So I ask you again, Mrs. Green, do you recognize this fabric?"

Karen clamped her lips together with a worried look on her face as she walked over to her haircutting area and opened the second drawer down. She pulled out a large square of fabric that was white with faded purple polka dots.

"What has she done…. what has my baby done?" she cried.

Detective Herrero looked at Jayne, she handed over the papers she was holding. The Detective handed the "Lost Horse" flyer to her. "We believe your daughter is responsible for the disappearance of this pony from Jayne Jordan's farm on the night of April, 29th or early morning of the 30th."

"No, that can't be. Caitlyn's pony doesn't look like this at all. He has a black hair on him, you know, not white…. well he has white on his face and legs, but the tail and hair on his neck are black, not blonde like this picture."

"Karen, I have seen my pony in your back yard. Our Gus has a white marking on his neck under the mane; that exact white marking is on the pony in your yard." Jayne looked at Detective Herrero and back to Karen and softly asked, "does Caitlyn have access to your black hair dye?"

Jayne and the Detective watched as Karen widened her eyes and looked briefly at thcm before she walked over to a closet and opened it. Her eyes darted around, looking at the various boxes on the shelves and she then selected a box and pulled it out. She put it on her workstation, closed her eyes and took a deep breath before opening the lid. She looked in and appeared to be counting.

Jayne watched the slow realization start to sink in and a look of sad horror began to appear on her face. "No! .....No!....... no, no, no, no, no....." Karen wailed. Jayne looked at Detective Herrero and walked over and put her arm around Karen's shoulders as Karen slowly sank to the floor.

~ ~ ~

Caitlyn pedaled her bike home as quickly as her tired legs could manage. Her mom was baking pork chops in the oven and just the thought of it was making her mouth water. She pedaled up her driveway past the car parked in the front. A hair cut client? This late on a Saturday?

She parked her bike behind the garbage can. Well, maybe if her mom was still with a client, Caitlyn would be able to grab a quick shower before dinner. She was taking off her helmet and walking to the door when she heard her mom shouting "No! .....No!"

Dropping her helmet on the porch she flung open the door and rushed in. She froze as the screen door slammed shut with a bang behind her. She had feared that her mom was being robbed or hurt somehow, but the horse trainer lady from down the street was comforting her; her mom had sunk to the ground and was weeping. Then when the screen banged, a uniformed police Detective turned around and when he saw her, he stood up tall and walked up to her.

"What happened to my mom?" She asked the Detective.

Then Caitlyn started to panic. The police. The horse trainer lady …. they know.

She looked past the detective at her mom and asked, "this is about the pony, isn't it?"

The trainer lady looked at her. She looked…. well, she looked quite mad, but a controlled mad. "That is my niece's horse in your back yard. We know what you did."

Caitlyn dropped her head and tears started falling as she whispered a small "yes."

The Detective walked up to her. "We would like to have a word with you and your mom down at the station." His comments were punctuated by a loud 'ding' sound that came from the kitchen.

~ ~ ~

The Detective steered Caitlyn to the unmarked patrol car and put her in the back seat with the doors locked. Jayne texted Beth and told the girls to come; they were taking Gus home. She then entered the kitchen and turned off the stove before everyone left and forgot about it. Mrs. Green was devastated and she didn't need her oven to catch fire and the house to burn down in addition to everything else going on tonight.

The two of them stood Mrs. Green up and Detective Herrero walked her to the patrol car and had her stand outside. "I have to get pictures of the pony and the box of hair dye, I will be right back." He pulled a little camera out of the console of his patrol car and shut the door again.

He disappeared through the gate into the yard and located the pony. Jayne saw the flash from the little camera illuminating the darkness on the other side of the wooden fence.

The Detective snapped photos and made sure to get the photo of the spot on his neck, then a few moments later went back into the house with his little camera. He collected the scraps of fabric. He already had the copies of Gus' photos showing the white mane and tail in his case file back at the station. The file also contained copies of the pony's registration papers and the yellow state of Florida Coggins paperwork, both of which had descriptions of the pony and proved ownership. He opened his cruiser door and put the fabric scraps in an evidence bag to bring back to the station.

"Mrs. Green, I don't think you are in a frame of mind to drive yourself to the station, so I will bring you with Caitlyn in the back of the cruiser. You should grab your purse and lock up." Karen nodded and went back in the house and reappeared with her handbag and keys. She locked up and the Detective held the car door open for her. As he was climbing into his seat in the unmarked car he looked at Jayne, "it is dark. Take your pony home, Mrs. Jordan."

They drove off and as the patrol car disappeared from sight, the girls emerged out of the darkness around the corner. They had taken turns riding and walking back from the preserve. Walking through the deep sand had made their legs ache. Monica was sound asleep on Copper's back, her little head bobbing in time with his steps as Melissa and Evelyn walked on each side holding her in the saddle so she wouldn't slip off.

Jayne looked at Beth, "go get Gus and let's go home."

# Chapter 15

It was well past dark by the time their happy little parade pulled into the driveway at Wildwood. Beth was riding Gus bareback using the purple halter and lead rope to steer. Monica was asleep in the truck with Jayne. The girls were riding the other three horses back with Sarah and Susan riding double.

They slowly made their way up the graveled driveway next to the paddock that Gus had disappeared from. The horses that the girls had put out in the paddock ran the fenceline and Gus pranced and nickered and whinnied the whole way up to the barn entrance. He was happy to be home.

Beth put Gus in his stall and brushed him down. She pulled a cream out of the cabinet in the tackroom and rubbed it on Gussie's pink sunburned nose that was crusty and peeling. He was missing both front shoes and he had a crack on one hoof. She picked the dirt out of his hooves and then painted them with hoof conditioner. He was munching on his hay when Beth went to the barn office and opened up the refrigerator. She returned with a can of root beer and stood in front of the stall.

Was this really her horse? She popped the can open and Gus looked up abruptly from his hay. He watched Beth put the can up to her lips and take a drink. He nickered, then flipped his head up and down with his lips flopping…. yes, this was HER pony. She went into the stall and held the can to the side of

Gussie's lips as he stuck his tongue out and licked and slurped the drink as she poured.

The girls rinsed off the horses, including the ones that had been put out in the paddock. They scraped the excess water off and put them in the stalls so they could eat their dinner.

Jayne handed a credit card to Beth. "I want you to order pizza for the girls and make sure everyone gets cleaned up. Wake Monica up and make sure she eats something and gets cleaned up too."

"Where are you going?"

"I am going to head to the police station to see what I can find out. I am leaving you in charge. If you need anything, call me and if you cannot get a hold of me for some reason, call Ms. Garcia at the corner. I will let her know that you are here while I run out. I shouldn't be long." She gave Beth a hug, "I should be back before ten I hope, they didn't go to the downtown station, they are at the local police substation on Busch Boulevard. I will be back as soon as possible."

Jayne returned at ten thirty and drove up the dark driveway. She saw a faint blue glow from a cellphone coming from the barn hallway as she drove past it up to the house.

She put the truck in reverse and backed up to the front of the barn and put on her bright headlights to shine down the barn hallway.

Beth put her arm up… "You are blinding me!"

Jayne turned the bright headlights off and went into the hallway. "You are in here?"

"I threw night hay to everyone and I wanted to see him and get pictures, but it is too dark. I will have to wait for morning." Beth yawned and Jayne brushed bits of hay out of her hair. Beth was dressed in a camouflage nightshirt that came almost to her knees, and she had slipped her feet into her rubber boots. Her hair had been braided into two pigtail braids with sparkly pink bows that were probably put there by Monica.

"Is this the new barn fashion?" Jayne asked.

Beth answered with a yawn.

"Let's go in and get some happy sleep tonight." Jayne put her arm around Beth and they walked down the hallway to the truck.

Jayne turned off her truck engine and shut the lights off. She locked the door and left the truck parked there in front of the barn as arm in arm the two of them walked the short distance to the house and climbed the stairs.

"Scrambled eggs and bacon in the morning…. make sure everyone is up early and I will fill you in on Caitlyn in the morning."

Jayne checked the time on her phone. "Matt will still be asleep. He is in London again and flies in to New York Monday, then he will be back home Wednesday," Jayne yawned. "I will have to call him in the morning. I called him before I went to the Green's house. He will be so ex...(yawn)…ited."

~ ~ ~

"Sarah, don't hoard all the bacon." Sarah looked up with a strip of the crispy meat hanging from her mouth as she passed the plate to her sister.

She finished chewing and swallowed, then reached to the pitcher of orange juice and topped off her glass. "I was looking online last night and they used to hang people who stole horses."

"Well that is not going to happen to Mrs. Green's daughter, they stopped doing that a long time ago. Please pass the juice." Jayne asked.

Beth was quiet.

Jayne continued, "Caitlyn confessed everything at the police station last night." Beth stabbed at her scrambled eggs but did not look up. Sarah was rapidly shoveling food in her face. Melissa and Susan put their forks down and looked at Jayne.

Monica took a long gulp of milk and put her cup down. She wiped her milk moustache on a napkin and asked, "who is Caitlyn?"

"The girl that stole Gus," replied Melissa who then shushed her so Jayne could continue.

"She walked here with a backpack that had a hammer, a pillowcase, a bottle of hair dye, rubber gloves and some petroleum jelly. She realized Gus didn't have a halter on, so she climbed over the fence and walked around in the dark until she found the halter and lead rope hanging at the gate. She haltered him and walked him down to the corner where the tree is and she tied him to a post."

"Then she used the hammer." Sarah squinted her eyes and nodded as she reached to her sister's plate and stole a piece of bacon. Her sister didn't notice.

"Yes, she used the hammer to pound the boards loose so that she could then use the hammer claws to pry the two top rails off the fence. She untied Gus and led him out over the bottom rail. She knew people would be looking for a horse with a very light mane and tail, so she had taken a bottle of hair dye and some rubber gloves from her mom's shop and she put hair dye in his mane and tail over on the side of the road. She smeared the petroleum jelly on his neck so the dye wouldn't get on his neck, and also put it around his tail. She then tied an old pillowcase around the tail so he wouldn't swish the tail and get dye on his sides…."

Evelyn interrupted "That was smart…devious smart."

"She had this planned out very well." Melissa agreed.

"Mrs. Jayne, why didn't she just dye his hair orange?" Monica asked.

They all looked at her.

Jayne answered her, "I guess Caitlyn isn't as smart as you are. That definitely would have been easier."

Monica gave a self-satisfied smiled and took another sip of milk.

"If she had used orange dye to make him a chestnut, she wouldn't have needed the petroleum jelly. I'll bet that was hard to wash off him later on." Susan pondered.

"Why black? Melissa wondered out loud. "I guess maybe her mom didn't have dye for red hair?"

"She did." Beth mumbled. She was visibly seething with anger.

Jayne watched Beth for a moment. Why was she in such a bad mood? Jayne thought she would be jumping for joy now that her pony was back home. She knew Beth had snuck out of the house at some time last night to go to the barn again. Jayne had awakened early and started pulling out the utensils to cook breakfast before the girls awakened, and had been startled when Beth sleepily came in the front door. She had some shavings stuck to her, so she must have laid in the stall with Gus for a bit during the night or early morning. Why was she acting this way?

Jayne continued with what she had learned at the station last night. "So...she dyed the hair by the road and put her rubber gloves and the bottle of dye back in her backpack and led Gus to her house. She washed him off and told her mom that someone had given him to her. That Sunday night, she went into her backpack to throw away the gloves and dye for the Monday garbage pickup and she realized that the bottle had somehow slipped out or she had forgotten it. She rode the bike back down here in the dark to look for it but couldn't find it."

"It was in the trash already when she came to look for it," Evelyn stated.

"NO!" Sarah wailed as the realization struck her. "I had evidence in my hands! I picked up that bottle and even pulled sticky hair off it!" She shook her head, "I threw evidence away; I thought it was garbage."

"No, you didn't throw it away, that lady selling the house threw it away. Remember she told us about how she raked

142

over the black gravel in the driveway? That must be where she was using the dye…. but you handed the bottle to the lady and she threw it away," Melissa recalled.

"The lady selling the house? You mean Ms. Miller?" Jayne thought back to the events of that horrible week. "You know, the day after Gus was taken she showed up at Mrs. Green's house to have black dye removed from her hair. She said she got it on her hands and phone."

"That bottle cracked and was leaking after Jahil stepped on it," Susan chimed in. The girls all nodded, except Beth. She sat back in her chair and was looking down. Her ears were red and Jayne though maybe her face was too.

"Caitlyn's father got injured and passed away a little over a year ago. He had always promised Caitlyn a horse like the one he had growing up and he used to tell her stories of his horse, who was a bay…so I guess that is why Caitlyn dyed his mane and tail black. Ever since her dad died, her mom has struggled to make enough money to keep their house and buy groceries. Caitlyn felt hopeless about ever being able to get a horse. She heard that Beth was getting a new horse, so she concocted the plan to take Gus and give him a good home."

"That is so sad." Susan exclaimed. Melissa nodded agreement.

Jayne continued, "well Caitlin was working at Foxhill and the day you guys saw her on Aristides Lane, she apparently hid up in a tree after throwing her bike into some bushes. She ripped the shirt coming out of the tree and that is the scrap you found. She was afraid that if you saw her again, you would recognize her so she cut the purple ends out of her hair and scraped paint off of her bike and she was going to repaint the bike a different color."

"Did she scrape the paint off with the hammer? Please tell me she used a hammer to do it, please, please, please!" Sarah pleaded.

Jayne squinted her eyes and looked at her, "What?... Never mind, I don't know how she scraped off the paint. She didn't tell us that part; it wasn't important."

"Yeeessssssss, it IS important; I need to know if I was right. I already feel like we are the WORST detectives ever born, so I want to know if I am right on THIS."

"Detective work does look so much easier on the TV shows." Melissa added.

Jayne laughed, "Ohhhhh Kayyyyyy.....I will see if I can find out that information for you. I am going to the courthouse this week when Caitlyn goes before the judge."

Beth put her hands on her ears and stood up so quickly she almost knocked the chair over. "I am tired of hearing that name… I don't want anyone to talk to me about her anymore. She nearly ruined MY life! How can you feel sorry for HER?" She then stomped across the living room and out the door slamming it closed so hard it bounced back open. Cora the dog had been laying on the porch and Beth almost tripped over her. Cora peeked into the house and trotted in. She jumped on the leather sofa and started to curl up but changed her mind and she trotted over to the table.

Jayne just stared after Beth. Evelyn got up and closed the door and sat back down. Everyone was quiet. Cora nudged Jayne's hand with her long, pointy collie nose and was rewarded with a slice of bacon.

"What are we going to do with the black hair?" Susan asked.

"Mrs. Green offered to help strip the color out. It will take a while and his color will never be exactly right until all new hair grows in, but we can get the black out of it eventually.

OK, girls, I think we are done here. Put the dishes in the sink then head out to the barn. I think I am going to longline just a few of the horses today instead of riding so I can finish early and take the rest of the day off. I think we need to celebrate with a long, trail ride. We will pack some lunch and we can picnic out on the preserve; we all need to unwind," - some more than others she thought to herself.

She looked at the remaining girls. "How does that sound?"

The girls cheered and Monica bounced.

~ ~ ~

Jayne guided them through the trails on Dallas who pranced the whole way. She hoped that the trail riding would teach this spirited horse to relax from time to time. It was Jayne's opinion that show horses just needed to unwind and have fun every once in a while, to help keep their minds fresh. She led them down the gravel ranger road to the cattle gate that would let them access the middle section of the preserve.

Beth dismounted and held the gate open for everyone to pass through and shut the gate behind them before remounting on Gus. The group had already begun to walk ahead and before she asked Gus to walk forward to catch up with them, she looked down at his neck and lifted the black mane. She gave a quick rub to his lucky white spot before leaning down and giving his neck a hug. She breathed in his wonderful, horsey scent as she let the tears flow.

Jayne scanned the horizon on the grassland. The cattle were further up their section of the preserve today and they could see them in the distance resting in the shade of some cypress trees. They looked like black and red blobs; Dallas snorted and kept looking at the cattle. They crossed without incident and the girls splashed the horses in the lake for a little bit without seeing any gators. Jayne waited on the shore on Dallas to watch; he had padded shoes on and she didn't want to get his feet wet. They then moved on through the fields that were dotted with pines and saw palmetto. Evelyn lost a stirrup and laughed when Magic plunged to a dead stop and swung his hips sideways to look and snort at a moving rock. It turned out to be a large gopher tortoise scurrying across the trail to her burrow.

They found a shady spot where they could tie the horses to branches as they sat down to eat lunch. All of the riders carried halters and lead ropes with them because Jayne wouldn't allow anyone to tie horses up using the bridles.

"Mrs. Jayne, I have to pee!"

Jayne looked around. "Monica, why don't you go behind that big palmetto bush over there......and don't squat close to the pointy leaves this time, I don't have bandages with me." She warned.

This was the most relaxed Jayne had felt in the weeks since Gus had disappeared. She glanced over at him. Wow, he looked ugly with that black hair. She muffled a little laugh.

Jayne's favorite color on a horse was bay, but this was just so ridiculously unnatural looking. Sometime this week she would have Mrs. Green come over and they would start to return Gussie's mane and tail to a more natural color for him.

Gus would probably have to skip the first show of the summer because that was coming up right after school let out; she didn't think he would have his original color back by then. It was against the rules to alter your horse's markings on the circuit for Morgan horses, so Gus could not legally show with black hair. It would most likely take several sessions to strip the hair, Mrs. Green had told her.

Beth wouldn't like that. Maybe she could convince her to focus on showing Dallas for the summer. Jayne shook her head. She had to stop thinking and just ….. enjoy the moment. Yes, enjoy the moment. She needed to let her brain relax, it had been working entirely to hard lately.

She listened to the quiet, it was just the soft sounds of an occasional nicker from one of the horses, a faint moo carried from the distant cows, a slight whisper of wind from above as the elusive breeze slid through the pine tree branches. It was so peaceful….and quiet.

"I farted," Sarah announced.

# Chapter 16

Jayne returned from the courthouse and felt as if a great weight had been lifted. She was happy for Beth and Gus; she was happy for herself; she was happy for Mrs. Green most of all.

Poor Mrs. Green, she was struggling with what her daughter had done and had pleaded with the judge to not send Caitlyn to Juvenile Detention. Jayne agreed. Caitlyn was smart, and resourceful and responsible. Jayne did not think putting her in jail …. with druggies and more hardcore juvenile thieves … would have a good outcome; it had the possibility of taking a basically good child and hardening her into something worse. But Caitlyn did have to have consequences for stealing an expensive show horse and much-loved pet.

The judge was lenient. She sentenced Caitlyn to a probation with many restrictions and a curfew, and many hours of community service that she needed to complete within a certain time frame. Jayne was happy for Mrs. Green who slumped in relief uttering "thank you-s" over and over.

A few days later, the first chemical strip of Gus' mane and tail took place and resulted in a smutty orangey-gray look. They would condition it and make another attempt at a later date. It would eventually lighten; she just didn't want it getting brittle from the chemicals because fragile hair would break, so this would have to be a slow process over many weeks.

Jayne finished her last ride of the day and handed the horse off to Bunny to untack and cool out and then put away. She sat at her office desk picking through a salad as she wrote down receipt amounts into her ledger and then filed the receipts in a folder. A rumble coming up the driveway caught her attention. A big horse trailer was pulling in. She covered the remaining salad and put it in the fridge. She had two more horses arriving for her to train. Business was definitely getting busy and she would soon have to put the 'no vacancy' sign on her barn.....or hire an assistant. Maybe when Beth was able to drive she could work afterschool for some spending money, Jayne pondered.

But what to do with Beth now. She was certainly happy to have Gus back and she spent time petting him, brushing him and riding him, but sometimes it was as if Beth didn't want to look at Gus with his black hair unless she had to, and there was an undercurrent of anger, always anger that she didn't want to talk about.

What would she do with Beth? Could Beth heal from this? Jayne would have to think carefully.

~ ~ ~

The following Saturday the girls were picking stalls. Jayne had cleared a spot in her schedule for a quick barn meeting and as she saw the car turning up her driveway, her stomach clenched. This was not going to be easy. She went out to meet the car and shuttled the people into the back door of the office, the door that faced outside of the barn towards the arena. A moment later, she exited the office from the other door that opened into the barn interior.

"Girls!" She called out. "Stop what you are doing and come here; I want to call a quick meeting."

150

One by one the girls wandered over. Melissa was the last one to join the gathering after she walked a wet horse out of the wash rack and quickly scraped the dripping water off. She put the horse back in his stall and shut the door just as everyone heard the horse groan and lay down to roll in the fresh bedding.

"Well, this is not going to be easy for me," she paused, "and I know it is not going to be easy for all of you, but I am hoping that long-term there will be positive benefits from what I am going to say."

The girls looked at each other nervously. "Is this bad news coming?" Evelyn asked. "You are not getting rid of the Pitchfork Princesses, are you?"

Several worried pairs of eyes watched her.

Jayne let out her breath and smiled. "No, we have added some extra horses over the last few weeks and it has added to the workload for everyone; I felt the need to add another girl for weekend stall duties."

The girls all looked at each other. "But that is a good thing, isn't it?" Susan asked.

Jayne watched as Melissa pushed her glasses up her nose. Melissa was smart, she knew there was more to the story to be revealed and she was just waiting.

Monica hopped up and down. "Who is it? I want to meet her!" Jayne put her hand on her head to settle her down, then walked over to the office and opened the door.

Mrs. Green walked out and turned around and beckoned to whoever was in the office behind her. Caitlyn slowly made her way out of the office. She couldn't make eye contact with anyone and twirled a piece of blonde hair that she had re-dyed the bottom a brilliant purple again.

The girls looked at each other, then looked at Beth. Beth's face was beet red and if it was possible for steam to come out of a person's ears like they do in children's cartoons, Jayne was sure that was about to happen to Beth.

Finally, Beth broke the silence with a loud. "NO" and she stalked down the hallway and out the back of the barn.

*To be continued…..*

Coming soon!

Turn the page to read an excerpt from

# CANDLES
# AND
# CARROT CAKE

book 2 in the Pitchfork Princess series

## (excerpt: Candles And Carrot Cake)

Beth tossed the popcorn in the bowl quickly and sprinkled it with the fake salt and rushed into the family room and plopped it on the coffee table in front of Uncle Matt and kept going. She went down the hallway and quickly entered the guest room where she stayed on the weekend visits and shut the door behind her.

She pulled her phone out of her pocket and quickly dialed Evelyn's number. "Evelyn, you mom is talking to Aunt Jayne, it sounds like they are talking about buying a horse!"

"Are you serious?!?!"

"Jayne went out onto the back porch to talk to her so I couldn't hear well, but I had my ear up to the door and I could hear bits and pieces."

"My mom is in the bathroom talking on the phone, I am going to listen at the door."

"Won't your dad catch you listening?"

"No, he and my brother are out night fishing out at the pier. It is just me and mom home until later. I will call you back."

Evelyn hung up without waiting for Beth to answer. She tiptoed down the hallway to her parents' room and pressed her ear up to the closed bathroom door. Her mom was definitely talking horses. She heard her birthday mentioned and then it sounded like her mom was going to look up plane ticket prices to New Hampshire for Thursday. That was interesting, a horse shopping trip in New Hampshire? What was that all about? The horse she wanted was Cleo at Wildwood Stables.

Evelyn was busy pondering this and at the last minute she realized her mom was ending the call. Evelyn spun around and tried to silently run out of the bedroom but she heard the knob turn and the bathroom door open so she stopped and turned. "Mom!"

Mrs. Knight was caught by surprise and her phone flew out of her hand; she juggled it around trying to catch it before it fell. Fortunately, she batted it towards the bed where it plopped down on the green comforter. "Heavens, you surprised me Evelyn. Is there something you want?"

"You mean besides my own horse?"

Her mom looked at her then glanced at the bathroom then back at Evelyn.

"I just came up here…. to ask … um, if I could have some money for the barn tomorrow. I want to order pizza delivered for lunch."

"Oh, I will check with your dad. I don't have any cash in my purse but maybe he can stop and pull some money from an ATM on his way home from the fishing trip. Why don't you run along and get your shower; you have final exams so I want you to get some studying done before you go to bed."

"Yes mama," Evelyn went to her room and grabbed her nightgown. She went into the bathroom and started the water in the shower and called Beth as the water warmed up.


"I think you are right, Beth. They were talking horses and I heard my birthday mentioned. It also sounded like my mom

155

is going to buy a plane ticket for your aunt to look at a horse for me up in New Hampshire?"

"I know what horse that is. My aunt has been looking at him for a while, she thinks he would make a good kid's horse."

"Is he as pretty as Cleo is?"

"He is pretty; he was at Nationals last year. My aunt was saying that he was a nice classic pleasure horse but she thinks he would look better as a Western horse. She has been thinking of getting him and seeing if she can switch him over."

"Why would she be looking at a Western horse for me?"

"You can be such a dummy sometimes; he IS an English horse. He is winning now as a kid's horse. Jayne just thinks he could look really nice Western too. She just likes having different options on the horses in her barn."

"Oh. Well, we need to find out what horse they are buying me. I have to jump in the shower and then study."

"Yeah, I need to study too, I am not looking forward to the final exam in history class on Monday. If I find anything out I will text you."

"About history?"

"No! About your birthday horse. You are so blonde."

"I am not the only blonde, you are too."

"I am barely blonde. Goodnight Evelyn."

98933118R00095

Made in the USA
Columbia, SC
03 July 2018